SLEEP
NO MORE

D1193673

SLEEP NO MORE

NO MORE

*Railway,
Canal & Other
Stories of the
SUPERNATURAL*

L.T.C. ROLT

INTRODUCTION BY SUSAN HILL

Cover image: Engine driver and stoker on the footplate
of a night train. (Mary Evans Picture Library)

First published in 1948
This edition published in 2010
Reprinted 2013

The History Press
The Mill, Brimscombe Port
Stroud, Gloucestershire, GL5 2QG
www.thehistorypress.co.uk

© The Estate of L.T.C. Rolt c/o Sonia Rolt, 1948, 1996, 2010

The right of L.T.C. Rolt to be identified as the Author
of this work has been asserted in accordance with the
Copyrights, Designs and Patents Act 1988.

All rights reserved. No part of this book may be reprinted
or reproduced or utilised in any form or by any electronic,
mechanical or other means, now known or hereafter invented,
including photocopying and recording, or in any information
storage or retrieval system, without the permission in writing
from the Publishers.

British Library Cataloguing in Publication Data.
A catalogue record for this book is available from the British Library.

ISBN 978 0 7524 5577 8

Typesetting and origination by The History Press
Printed in Great Britain by TJ International Ltd, Padstow, Cornwall

AUTHOR'S NOTE

The characters in these stories are entirely fictitious and bear no relation whatsoever to any actual person, living or dead. The settings of certain of the stories are, however, based on actual places, but I would assure any readers who may succeed in identifying them that I do not attribute to such places or to their inhabitants any supernatural or sinister quality.

L.T.C.R.

CONTENTS

INTRODUCTION

Few things are more disturbing, on reading an account of some dreadful catastrophe, than the chill which accompanies the realization that we ourselves could well have been – perhaps almost were – actually there. The terrorist bomb destroys a building we frequently visit; we narrowly miss boarding a plane that crashes on take-off; we often walk through the isolated beauty spot where the battered body of a traveller was discovered yesterday. Reading of events which happened centuries ago, or in far-distant and unfamiliar places, makes nothing like such an impact.

The ghost story, and its close relative, the tale of the supernatural, has exactly the same power to disturb us most when set in a world recognizable, and even familiar to us. The point is in the juxtaposition between this ordinary, apparently 'real' place, full of reassuringly solid objects like railway trains and racing cars, and people such as phlegmatic policemen and taciturn farm labourers, and that which is bizarre, strange, frightening, other-worldly and unaccountable.

L.T.C. Rolt knew this very well, and one of his greatest strengths as a writer of stories of the supernatural is his ability to lead us, in an easy, relaxed way, into an apparently ordinary and pleasant world, where we may see trains passing through tunnels, people out walking, canal boats mooring for the night, men going about their daily work in fields and down mines and eating their dinners off solid oak tables; it is only after he has settled us comfortably in the midst of it all, that he begins to slide the carpet gently from under our feet, slowly, slowly, so that we feel just a little uneasy, knowing something is wrong, uncertain quite what. Then the screw begins to turn – *as we knew perfectly well it would.*

Tom Rolt was a trained engineer, a railway enthusiast and the owner of a narrow boat in which he navigated the inland waterways of England and Wales; as a child he grew up with a passionate love of solitude, and of the Black Mountains on the Welsh Borders. He loved poetry, particularly that of Henry Vaughan, Thomas Traherne and W.B. Yeats, and was something of a mystic himself, a reflective, inward-looking and somewhat taciturn man, a self-taught historian and a natural philosopher. He also restored and drove old cars, and founded the famous Prescott Hill Climb near his home in Gloucestershire, of which he writes in the tight-knit and exciting ghost story included here, 'New Corner'. He knew well and admired greatly the sort of men he believed were the backbone of his country, those who built the ships and the railway trains and stood on their footplates, manned the signal-boxes and the locks, mined the iron, coal and china clay, quarried the stone, and grafted on the land. Almost all of them appear in *Sleep No More*, a collection not only of splendidly traditional, quintessentially English stories of ghosts and the supernatural, but also of the passions which informed Tom Rolt's life and work. Indeed, anyone wanting to know and understand him could well begin here; the book encapsulates him.

There is nothing at all experimental about this collection, which will delight lovers of the classic form of supernatural story which stretches back into the seventeenth century, but which reached its heyday in the writings of Victorians. Rolt looks firmly backward, owes the style and shaping of his stories to the traditions of the past, and is proud to do so. He was an admirer of the great M.R. James and it shows, but he is also and firmly his own man; these are not derivative imitations.

He is best of all in the setting of scenes and the conjuring up of atmosphere. He adds detail slowly and patiently, building it up in a masterly way to the unnerving climax. We always know what we are in for when we enter this world of melancholy valleys, lonely moors, isolated farms and inns, on lowering winter afternoons and pitch-black nights, and we let ourselves in for it most willingly, so as to be frightened delightfully. But we are always at one comforting remove from the source of whatever terror grips the protagonists. Rolt's method is to allow us to look on helplessly as the narrator, or subject, of the story approaches and encounters the worst, and is either overcome by it, literally unto death, or is driven insane, or at the very least, is left haunted for life by the terrible memory.

These are not pure ghost stories, for those 'things' which drive one to madness and death are often satyrs, demons and other nameless, hideously shaped creatures from the netherworlds. A ghost is the spectre – and sometimes the voice, or even smell – of a human being who was once alive and is now dead, yet who returns to haunt a particular place or person; and a ghost is not necessarily evil, just as a ghost story is not necessarily frightening, but may be sad, moving or even funny. There is occasionally a touch of melancholy, or wistfulness, in L.T.C. Rolt's stories, but never laughter, except of a demoniacal kind. These are dark tales. The sense of evil and dread and doom is wonderfully conjured up, powerfully gripping. Anyone who has been into the Black Mountains of Herefordshire and Radnorshire will know that though their atmosphere is usually of the greatest tranquility, beauty and spirituality, it can also be one of dread, menace, depression and foreboding. I do not know of any writing that conveys this better than the wonderful story 'Cwm Garon'.

There are plenty of tales of railway hauntings, but no one has better described the lonely life of the old-fashioned signal-box keeper in a bleak and remote place more evocatively than Rolt, in 'The Garside Fell Disaster', just as no one has well succeeded in capturing the air of dankness and dreariness of lonely canals on gloomy, misty late afternoons in winter. We feel something is bound to happen at any moment, in such places (or at the very least, must surely have happened once, and that that something was terrible).

The stories in *Sleep No More* are not for sunny days and happy company; they are for reading by the fireside in winter, with a gale howling round the chimney, or on long, lonely train journeys, or in a bedroom at a remote county inn. They are for delight – the sort of delight that comes to the one who, while deeply immersed in them, would prefer, thank you, not to glance over his shoulder.

SUSAN HILL

THE MINE

There was a high west wind over the Shropshire March – a boisterous, buffeting wind that swept down the slopes of the Long Mynd and over the Vale of Severn to send November leaves whirling through the darkness from the mane of Wenlock Edge. It cried about the walls of the 'Miner's Arms' at Cliedden, hurling sudden scuds of rain to rattle like flung gravel against the window-panes. It was a night to make men glad of the warmth and cheer of the fireside.

'Why is it called Hell's Mouth? Ah, now that's a long story, that is.'

With a natural sense of drama, the old man paused to allow the interest of his audience to quicken. He took a deep and noisy draught from the mug which was mulling on the hob, filled a yellowing clay with fine black shag from a battered tin and lit it with an untidy spill of newspaper which he thrust between the bars of the grate. Then at last, settling himself more comfortably in the chimney-corner, be began his tale.

'If you got here afore dark, maybe you noticed the old mines on the hill yonder. Well, they were lead-mines, and were working up to – let me see – fifteen years ago; all but the one right on top of the hill, that is, and that's been closed these fifty years. Now, this be the mine you've been on about, though in the old days it were called Long Barrow Mine because there's a great mound up there which they do say was some old burial-place when Adam was a boy-chap. I never heard tell of anyone who could say rightly who were buried there, although folks who know about such things have set to a-digging there many a time, but never got much forrarder. Not that any of them stayed at it very long. It seemed to get on their nerves like, for it be a queer lonely place up there even in day-time, and, though rabbits do swarm on these hills, you'll never see a one there, nor any other natural creature neither. Knowing what I know, I don't blame them for packing up.

'Now, in the old days when my father were a young man there was a horse-tram road – Ginny Rails we call 'em – between the mines and Cliedden Wharf down here in the valley. This wharf was the end of an old arm that used to run to the Shroppie Cut by Fens Moss, but it has been dry now these many years, and you wouldn't see no sign of it today save you knew where to look. About the time I was born the railway came, and soon after that they made a steam tramway up to the mines.

They kept the same narrow gauge, only the track were different – better laid, and went a deal further round, to ease the grade. They still used horses then to draw the trams up the branch roads from the mines ready for the engine to pick up, and this were my first job as a nipper, walking one of these horses up from Half-way Mine to the main road. Then, when I was twenty or thereabouts, I got the job of firing on one of the engines, and proud as Punch I was. She'd seem pretty queer to you folks nowadays, but she was a grand little engine in them days, and I used to keep her brass Bristol fashion, and the copper band round her funnel shone like my mother's kettle.

'It was about this time – one Michaelmas – that the trouble started in Long Barrow Mine. I can remember it as plain as if it were yesterday. We had our shed up there then, and we'd just come up with our last load of empties, unhooked, and were running the engine into shed, when the chaps came up off shift. Now, the path from the mine down the hill led past the door of our shed, and I had dropped my fire and was having a last look round just to see as everything was right for the night as they come walking by. Usually they would be a-chattering, joking and calling to each other, for they were a merry lot, but this night they were quiet like or talking hushed to each other, and this was the first thing that struck me as being a bit queer. So when one of them that was a cousin of mine – Joe Beecher his name was – come walking by, I called out to him to know what they was all acting so glum about. He turned back into the shed and told me what the trouble was. It was fast falling dark by this time, but I can see his face now in the light of my fire, which was still a-glowing between the rails by the door.

'They had struck a new vein just about that time and it seems that Joe and his mate had been working on this new level. Mind you, it wasn't like the mines you know of to-day, for there was only about fifteen men at the most below ground. Well, at midday they knocked off for a bite of "Tommy", and started walking back to the road to join their mates. When they got half way, he said, his mate Bill remembered he'd left his tea-can behind, and set off back to fetch it while Joe went on and joined the others. They had a laugh about Bill when he was so long finding his can, but when snapping time was nearly up and still no sign of him, Joe said he got a bit worried, and set off down the level to see what had happened to him. He got to the end, and then he said he came over horrid queer because Bill wasn't there at all, so that he felt scared of the dark and the hush there, and hollered out for the others to come down. So they came and looked, too, and sure enough there was nothing to be seen of Joe's mate. There'd been no fall to bury him, and of course there was no other way out of the level. They just stood there for a moment very quiet like, and then set off back to the road again as fast as they could. Joe said something seemed to be telling him that the sooner he cleared out the better for him, and he reckoned the others must have felt that way, too. He finished up by saying something that sounded a bit crazed to me at the time, about the darkness being angry. Anyway, none of them durst set foot in that level for a long while after that.'

The old man paused, drained his beer-mug, and, sucking the drooping fringe of his moustache, seemed to ruminate sadly over its emptiness.

His mug replenished and his reeking pipe re-lit, he settled himself once more and resumed his tale.

'Nothing else happened for a twelve-month or more, except that they had to give up the new level because no one would work there. But there come a time when they'd worked out the veins on the old levels, and it was a matter of opening up the new level again, seeing as it was very rich, or shutting down altogether. Things had quieted down a bit by this, mind, but for all that they had to give the chaps more pay afore they'd agree to go back.

'It must have been a fortnight or more after they'd started on the new level again, that we were up there waiting for a return load of trams, and had gone into the winding-house to have a word with Harry Brymer, who was engine-man there in them days. Died ten year ago up at his daughter's at Coppice Holt, he did. It was an old beam winder as was there then, gone for scrap a long time back, though you can still see the engine-house plain as can be on top of the hill, while the old chimney be a landmark ten mile away on a clear day.

'Well, Harry was telling us how they'd had nothing but trouble ever since they'd started on the new level – nothing much, mind, but just enough to make the men nervy and talk of an ill luck on the place, although Harry said he reckoned nothing to it for his part.

'It was while we were talking to Harry, leaning over the guard rails round the drum and having a smoke, that the bell wire started to play the monkey. There was no such new-fangled notion as electricity in those days, of course, and the signal for winding was a bell as was hung on the wall and rung from the shaft bottom by a wire cable working through pulleys and guides. Well, it was this cable that started a jangling to and fro in the guides just enough to set the bell moving, but not enough to ring it proper. The three of us stopped our clacking and stood dumbstruck watching this bell moving and the cable jerking. And somehow it felt queer standing there in the half-light watching it and waiting for it to make up its mind, like, whether to ring or not. Then all on a sudden it starts ringing like mad, and kept on, too; so Harry started winding while we went to the doorway to look for the cage, for by that time we had a notion as summat was up. When her came there was only one man on her and that was Joe Beecher; I just caught a sight of his face as he come up and I'll never forget the way he looked. He never said nor shouted nothing, nor even saw us, but almost afore the cage stopped he was off and away across the yard, and we could see him running for dear life over the waste mound and along the hill-side. And as he ran he kept looking back over his shoulder and then running the harder, for all the world as though Old Nick hisself were after him. Then he got to Dyke Wood, and we lost sight of him because it was that dark under the trees.

'Now this gave Harry and me a pretty turn, I can tell you, but that was nothing to my mate. When we were watching Joe a-running he lets out a yell like a screech owl and then cries out loud, "Run, run, for Christ's sake!" When we couldn't see Joe no more we turned to look at him and he'd gone down all of a heap on the floor. We reckoned then he must have seen summat as we missed, but it was some hours afore he came round, and a week or more afore he could talk plain. Even then it very near set him off again in the telling. I can tell you that if I'd known then what it was he saw, I'd never have gone down that mine as I did with several others as had been working above ground. Even as it was, it was a bit strange, to say the least, going down in that cage and wondering what we were going to see when we got to the bottom.   .

'I know that none of us expected what we did find when we had stepped out of the cage and walked off down the new level – just the quiet and the dark – not a sign of a mortal soul. I understood then what poor Joe had meant about the darkness being angry. I'm not an educated man; if I were maybe I could find a better word for the feeling there was down in that mine. It just told me pretty plain that we weren't wanted down there, and the sooner we cleared out the better for us. I reckon the others must have felt the same thing, for we soon set off back to the cage, walking pretty smart for a start and finishing at a run, so that we fell a-jostling back into the cage like so many sheep into a pen, and mighty glad we were to see daylight, I can tell you.'

The old man paused, rubbing his hands nervously one over the other and drawing his chair nearer to the fire as though suddenly chilled.

'We found Joe Beecher in Dyke Wood,' he went on, 'at the bottom of the old quarry as there is there. We covered up his face quick with a coat. I didn't fear God nor man in them days, but it were too much for me, and it didn't seem right that a mortal face should take that shape.

'Meanwhile, of course, my mate was took pretty bad. He'd just lie on his bed come day go day and not a word to anyone, but in the night he'd start shaking all over and crying out something terrible, same as he'd done the first time in the engine-house. He nearly drove his old woman crazy, too, but after a time he quieted down until one day he was man enough to tell us what it was he saw.

'Then he said that when the cage came up there was something crouched a-top of it, holding on to the cables. He couldn't see it very plain, he said, not half as clear as he could see Joe even in the half-light, but it had a human shape, he thought, even if it did seem terrible tall and thin, and it seemed to be a kind of dirty white all over, like summat that's grown up in the dark and never had no light. When the cage stopped it come down and made after Joe as quick and quiet as a cat after a sparrow. He could hear Joe's running plain enough across the yard, he said, but this thing made never a sound, though it went fast enough and was catching up on him, so that when he got to the edge of the wood it looked as if it was reaching out for him with its arms.

'Well I can't tell you no more. No one never went down that mine again, and we cut the cage ropes and the guides and covered over the mouth of the shaft with girt great old timbers all bolted fast. A bit foolish, maybe you'll think, but when we heard my mate's tale we fancied, like, that something might come a-crawling up. Any road, that's how it come to be named Hell's Mouth instead of Long Barrow. For myself I reckon hell be too good a name for it. Bible says hell be fire and brimstone, but at any rate fire is something I can understand and I could abide it better than the dark and the quiet down there.'

THE CAT RETURNS

It was certainly not a very cheerful start for a honeymoon, Steven reflected as they groped their way hand in hand up the dark lane. It was fortunate that both he and Myrtle possessed a strong sense of humour and so could appreciate the humorous side of their predicament. It was just like the conventional opening of a mystery film; a newly wed couple, a pitch-dark night of rain and wind, the car breaking down miles from anywhere, and now this tramp through the storm in search of shelter. How many times had he not sat in the warmth of a cinema and watched on the screen precisely this same sequence of events?

But whereas the benighted couple of the film story invariably arrived at some sinister, moated grange, candle-lit and cobwebbed, the light towards which Steven and Myrtle groped their way came from a far less romantic source. It shone from beneath the portico of a house which would have been described by a house agent as 'ultra-modern', and which presented to the narrow lane an angular façade of smooth stucco and gaping steel-framed windows. In response to Steven's ring there appeared on the doorstep no frightening or sinister figure, but an insignificant little man who, in fact, was undoubtedly scared by them. Obviously the manservant, Steven decided, as he explained their plight. The other seemed to be reassured by his explanation, for he opened the door wider and ushered them in, saying as he did so, in a nervous, jerky manner:

'Come in, come in, do, only too pleased to help you. It's a dreadful night to be stranded, and you must stay here, of course.'

He insisted on helping them out of their sodden coats, which done he showed them into the lighted room from which he had obviously emerged. It was expensively but tastelessly furnished in a style in keeping with the rest of the house, and a cheerful wood fire burned in the grate.

Their host had evidently been settled in an easy chair by the fireside, for the cushions were disturbed, a decanter, siphon and glass stood on a small table beside it, and a newspaper, hurriedly thrown aside, lay crumpled on the carpet. He motioned them to be seated.

'Have you dined?' he enquired, and without waiting for an answer, continued in the same nervous monotone: 'Let me get you sandwiches, I am afraid it is the best I can offer you at this hour.' He silenced their protestations with a quick gesture: 'No, no. I insist, it's no trouble, I assure you. I will get fresh glasses, too, and you must join me in a drink. You must both be chilled after being out on such a night, and the whisky will do you good.' He walked to the door.

When their host had left the room Steven glanced enquiringly at Myrtle.

'What do you make of him?' he whispered.

She smiled. 'I think the cat's away,' she replied, 'and the mouse is playing. Sitting in master's chair and drinking master's whisky. No wonder we scared him. I'm surprised he didn't turn us away, but he's evidently decided to try to bluff it out. Obviously he's alone in the house, for if there was someone in the kitchen to cut the sandwiches he'd have been back by now. Most likely he's making up a bed for us, too.' She paused and clutched his arm. 'What's that?'

Steven chuckled and pointed to the telephone.

'It's all right, my sweet, you're not in the haunted grange, remember; everything's terribly dull and civilized, it was only the 'phone tinkling; the sort of funny little noise it makes when the exchange connects up by mistake and finds that it's a wrong number just in time. There it goes again. Perhaps there's something wrong with the bell, and it really is someone trying to ring through. The mouse doesn't seem to be coming back, so perhaps I'd better answer it.'

He picked up the receiver, but could only hear a confused whirring and crackling, like wireless atmospherics. Thinking that after all it must be a false alarm, caused no doubt by the wind in the wires, Steven was about to hang up when the noises suddenly ceased and a male voice asked abruptly:

'Is Hawkins there?'

The tone was hoarse and querulous, obviously that of an old man. Steven thought rapidly. He felt sure that Hawkins must be their nervous host, and he had a shrewd suspicion that the caller was none other than his absent master.

'Yes,' he replied, without appreciable hesitation. 'If you wouldn't mind holding on a moment, I'll go and find him.'

'Don't trouble,' said the voice. 'Just tell him I shall return in the morning. He'll understand.'

'Who is it speaking?' asked Steven, but there was no reply. He listened for a moment more, then set the receiver down and turned to Myrtle.

'You were quite right, darling; our good host, whose name is Hawkins incidentally, is certainly the mouse in this establishment. The cat has just 'phoned up to say he'll be back in the morning. Sounded a peppery old devil, too. No wonder poor Hawkins is a bundle of nerves. He wouldn't wait for me to fetch him to the 'phone; gave no name either, and I must say I was expecting him to ask who the devil I was and what I was doing in his house.'

'Hush,' whispered Myrtle, laying a hand on his arm. 'He's coming back.'

Steven turned towards the door as their host reappeared bearing a plate of sandwiches and two more glasses upon a tray, which he set down beside the decanter.

'Please help yourselves,' he invited, as he moved the table towards them and filled the three glasses generously.

Steven raised his glass.

'Good health,' he toasted, 'and many thanks. You've saved our lives; but for you we should most likely be spending a wretched night in the back of the car.'

The other smiled wanly in acknowledgment, but made no reply. Steven sat down. There was an awkward pause, broken only by the sound of the rain lashing at the windows, and the ticking of the clock on the mantelshelf, which asserted itself for the first time.

This is tricky, Steven was thinking. I've got to tell him about the 'phone message somehow so that he won't suspect I've tumbled to his little game. I wonder how he'll take it; bluff it out, I expect, and make some excuse for not being able to put us up after all, or perhaps he'll make a clean breast of it and let us stay on condition we make a get-away before the old boy gets back!

He covertly studied the other; the pallid face so lacking in expression, the ever-restless hands, and the dark nondescript clothes. Every feature was self-effacing except the eyes. They were pale blue and slightly protuberant and like the hands they were never still. For a moment Steven intercepted their roving gaze, and somehow behind their superficial nervousness it seemed to him that there lurked a sort of furtive malevolence like that of a cowed but dangerous animal.

At length he cleared his throat and took the plunge.

'Are you Mr Hawkins, by any chance?' he asked diffidently. He had expected the other to make some little show of surprise, but if he had suddenly whipped out a revolver the effect could not have been more startling. The man shrank back in his chair, and the hand that held his glass shook so violently that the whisky slopped over on to his knees. Poor devil, thought Steven; the old boy must be a tartar: for the other seemed to be quite panic-stricken by this innocent question and to be fighting hard to control himself.

'How did you know?' he managed to blurt out at last.

Steven smiled reassuringly.

'Quite simple,' he explained. 'While you were outside the 'phone went, and someone asked for a Mr Hawkins. I thought it must be you, and offered to go and find you, but whoever it was wouldn't wait, but just told me to say that he would be coming in the morning. I asked for the name, but he'd evidently hung up on me by then. He sounded to me like an oldish man.'

While he had been speaking the other had gulped down his whisky, which seemed to pull him together somewhat for he replied with some show of composure.

'Of course – stupid of me – I was expecting the call, but for a moment I was startled because I couldn't think how you had found out my name.'

You're lying, and clumsily, too, thought Steven, you never expected that call, and now you're trying to bluff it out. But why get in such a panic; the old boy can't be as bad as all that; still, I'd better give you a good chance to get out of it, so he said tactfully:

'I'm so sorry if I startled you; perhaps, too, this 'phone message upsets your plans. If it makes it inconvenient now for you to let us stay, please don't hesitate to say so, and we'll be on our way. After all, we must be somewhere near a village, and if I might use your 'phone maybe I could ring the local pub.'

'No, no,' the other insisted, to their surprise. 'I won't hear of your turning out again on such a night, and besides,' he added, with a glance at Myrtle, 'it's a good two miles to the nearest inn, and it's a poor place at that.'

'Don't worry about me, please,' Myrtle insisted. 'I'm perfectly prepared to do what my husband says. Besides,' she added, with a smile, 'after your excellent whisky a two-mile walk has no terrors for me.'

Their polite protestations only made it obvious, however, that their strange host, despite his nervousness, was almost pathetically eager for them to stay, so they were not loath to agree.

There followed another strained interval, during which Myrtle and Steven both made valiant attempts to draw their host into conversation by discovering some topic in which he took an interest. He seemed quite distrait, however, and expressed no opinion of his own till at length:

'I am afraid I am a poor host tonight. Business worries, you know, get on one's mind. No doubt you are both tired after your journey and your room is ready, so if you wish I'll show you to it.'

They accepted readily, being in truth dog-tired, so with renewed thanks for his hospitality, they followed their host up the stairs. He led them to a large, bright room as featureless as the rest of the house and bid them good night.

'Well, darling, what do you make of your mouse now?' asked Steven as they undressed.

'Probably he knows that the old boy won't be back till late tomorrow morning,' she conjectured, 'so he's decided to stick to his guns and get us out of the house early tomorrow. But why he should seem so scared and yet be so anxious for us to stay I can't imagine.'

'Anyway,' Steven concluded as he jumped into bed, 'we've got a roof over our heads and a comfortable bed, that's the main thing, so let's forget about poor Mr Hawkins and his worries till the morning.'

A wan dawnlight was filtering through chinks in the window curtains when Steven suddenly awoke, and he glanced at the luminous dial of his watch. It was four-thirty. The wind had fallen and the house was utterly quiet. He was usually a very sound sleeper, and now he had an uneasy feeling that some strange instinct, whether prompted by dream or reality he knew not, must have caused him to awaken thus suddenly and at such an unearthly hour. Yet there was no sound, and at his side Myrtle slept peacefully enough.

As he lay on his back, wide-eyed in the darkness, he suddenly recalled a Christmas house-party he had once attended. He remembered how, one night, they had sat round the fire and held a competition to decide who could describe the most terrifying apparition.

They had conjured up a grim company of headless knights and malevolent cowled monks, but the winner had described a most insignificant little ghost in modern dress, which had on a sudden revealed a face, if face it could be called, that was innocent of any feature, a blank cranium of flesh more terrible in its inhumanity than any human face, however grotesque, could ever have been.

It seemed to Steven that this house and its solitary occupant, so prosaic the previous evening, had now taken upon themselves some of the horror of that featureless face, so empty did they seem of any human warmth or character.

He felt that the silence of the house had become charged with a sort of ominous expectancy. It was like the hush that falls before a storm breaks, when even the birds are silent.

The tension became so unbearable that he felt he must cry out, and might have done so had he not been forestalled by someone close at hand.

Once as a boy he had shot a hare, and this sound recalled vividly the horror he had felt then as he heard the thin terrible scream of terror and pain which the helpless thing had given before it died.

There followed a few moments' stillness before he thought he heard a just audible click as though the sneck of a door, closed with infinite stealth, had sprung home. Then there came, undoubtedly from the next room, a confused choking and bubbling noise, very terrible to hear.

This was too much for Steven. He clambered stealthily out of bed, bent over Myrtle for a moment to assure himself that she still slept, and then groped his way to the door.

The sight that met his eyes when he switched on the light in the next room was one destined to remain with him in all its horrid detail for the rest of his life. It was a scene of Grand Guignol. The man Hawkins lay on his back in the bed, his blue eyes no longer restless, but staring fixedly upward. His throat was cut and he was obviously dead, for his choking had ceased. A broad crimson stain had welled up over the coverlet, and on the floor, just out of reach of the limp fingers of his dangling right hand, lay an open razor. The handle was of ivory and upon it were engraved the initials 'A.M.'

The morning was well advanced when Steven and Myrtle returned to the house with the local constable, a stolid and imperturbable countryman, whose company they found oddly reassuring. To their relief he seemed to have accepted without question the explanation of their presence in the house. He left them to wait below while he stumped ponderously up the stairs to investigate.

'Well, he's done for himself right enough, as you say,' he announced, when he eventually rejoined them. 'Just the very same as his master done a year ago.' He shook his head. 'A queer business – but, then, they was a queer couple, we could never make head nor tail of them.'

Steven threw Myrtle a significant glance.

'Do you really mean to say that his master did this, too?'

'That's right,' nodded the other. 'Professor Arthur Morgan, that was his name. Funny old gent. Lived abroad most of his life, so they said, and came here to retire. Had this house built, he did, right away from the village, because he reckoned he didn't want no company. Lived here alone with this feller Hawkins for the best part of four years and then, as I said before, one fine morning a year ago, there he was dead in his bed.' He drew his forefinger across his throat in a significant gesture. 'Left everything to Hawkins he did, house and all, and here Hawkins have lived all by hisself till now.'

'Must have got on their nerves, I suppose, living so much alone,' was all the comment Steven could think of. Then as the thought occurred to him he added, 'I suppose we shall have to attend the inquest, which is going to be an infernal nuisance.'

The policeman's eyes twinkled benevolently as he glanced at Myrtle. 'Well,' he said judicially, 'I reckon we can manage without you, if you and I don't go a-talking too much about it. After all, you won't have no more honeymoons together, so you'd best make the most of this one. You've had trouble enough already getting mixed up in this business.' He jerked his head aloft.

Steven grinned broadly and took Myrtle's hand in his.

'That's damned decent of you, Constable, I must say,' he exclaimed. 'Oh, and by the way, that reminds me, our car is still stranded by the roadside where we left it last night. I must get a garage to send out and collect it.' He walked towards the 'phone. 'It would be all right for me to ring them from here, wouldn't it?'

The constable smiled and shook his head.

'I'm afraid you won't do no good there, sir,' he answered. 'I know because my daughter works on the exchange; Mr Hawkins gave orders for it to be cut off six months or more ago.'

BOSWORTH SUMMIT POUND

With the exception of the lock-keepers in their lonely cottages by the Cold Bosworth and Canonshanger locks, and of the infrequent boatmen who navigate its narrow, tortuous course, very few people are familiar with the little-used North Midland section of the Great Central Canal. Many have crossed over it and perhaps caught a brief glimpse of its still, reed-fringed waters as they hurried northward by those great main road and rail routes which stride so arrogantly across the Midland Shires. Yet they are seldom sufficiently interested to enquire whither this forgotten water road leads. Again, antiquaries and those who make it their hobby to 'collect' village churches will be familiar with the splendid broach spire of St Peter's, Cold Bosworth, which, standing four-square to the winds of the wolds, is such a prominent local landmark. But when they stand in the nave to admire the remarkable fourteenth-century rood-screen or the delicate tracery of the clerestory windows, they do not realize that the waters of the Great Central Canal lie directly beneath their feet. In fact, the church of St Peter stands upon that great belt of limestone which extends from the Dorset coast to the Yorkshire border, and which here forms the central watershed of England. As a glance at a contoured map will show, the erosion of the small streams which may carry the rain-water from the church roof to the Humber, the Wash or the Bristol Channel has considerably narrowed the ridge at this point. Consequently it was here that the canal engineers decided to cut the watershed by a tunnel over a mile long. Just above the lock called Bosworth Top, and within a few hundred yards of the churchyard wall, the canal disappears underground, but as both lock and tunnel portal are hidden in the thick undergrowth of Bosworth wood, a stranger standing in the churchyard would be unaware of their existence.

Before he leaves the precincts of St Peter's, I would draw the visitor's attention to a tombstone standing on the north side of the churchyard. The stone itself is of no particular merit, while it bears no inscription to attract the eye of the collector of curious epitaphs. It may therefore easily escape notice. Although a frequent visitor to the church, I must confess that I never noticed it myself until my attention was drawn to it by Fawcett's story. It was then that I appreciated that the inscription, though simple, is, after all, somewhat singular. It reads:

'Here lies the body of
MARY GRIMSDEN,
of Canonshanger in this parish,
Aged 25 years.

Here lies also the body of
JOHN FORTESCUE LOFTHOUSE
of Coppice Farm, Cold Bosworth.
Died 14th February 1841, aged 31 years.

"In death they were not divided."'

The fact that the date of Mary Grimsden's death is not given might conceivably be due to an error on the part of the village mason, but that two ostensibly unrelated persons should be buried in a common grave and accorded an epitaph usually reserved for those who have enjoyed many years of conjugal felicity should strike the reflective as peculiar.

Henry Fawcett was one of those men who love 'messing about in boats', to use a popular phrase, and as he was a man of independent means with no domestic ties (he was a confirmed bachelor), he was able to indulge his passion to the full throughout his long lifetime. Although I accompanied him on several occasions, even I had no idea of the extent of his voyaging until, after his death, there came into my possession a number of manuscript volumes in which, minutely detailed in his cramped characteristic hand, he had kept a complete record of his travels. From this it appeared that there were few harbours in the Mediterranean or along the north-western seaboard of Europe with which he was not familiar. As may be imagined, the log recorded many adventures, some of them experiences that would have induced many less intrepid sailors to leave the sea for solid earth. There is thus something oddly ironical in the fact that a man who, single-handed, could ride out an equinoctial gale in the Bay of Biscay without a qualm should have been scared almost out of his wits on the narrow landlocked waters of the Great Central Canal at Cold Bosworth in the heart of the English Midlands.

It happened in 1932, on what was fated to be his last voyage. In the autumn of '28, Fawcett had returned to England a sick mam. He lay in hospital all that winter, and when at last he was able to get about again he realized bitterly that his sea-going days were over. But he would not leave the water. 'I shall have to stick to fresh water', he told me ruefully. He sold his yawl *Deirdre* and bought one of those long, narrow canal-boats which he proceeded to convert into a comfortable motor-driven house-boat. The last time I saw him was during the winter of '31 when he had a snug berth on the Trent and Mersey Canal. He then seemed in good health and spirits, and told me of his intention to move south in the spring. I had no further news of him until the following June when I heard, with some surprise, that his boat, the *Wildflower*, was up for sale. A week or so afterwards I read the announcement of his death in *The Times*.

Because Fawcett recorded his last voyage in his usual scrupulous manner, and thanks to my intimate knowledge of the district, it has been easy for me to reconstruct the story of his experience at Cold Bosworth. He was accompanied by a friend unknown to me who is referred to in the log as Charles. The journey from the Trent and Mersey to the Great Central was accomplished in good weather and without any untoward incident, and a fine May morning found them beginning the long climb up the Canonshanger locks towards Cold Bosworth summit level. Charles, it appears, had to return to London for a couple of days on business, so it was agreed that when they reached a convenient mooring-point, Fawcett should await his return. Because it is connected by branch line with Rugby, Cold Bosworth was selected. Fawcett consulted the lock-keeper at Canonshanger as to a convenient mooring and was advised to tie up below Bosworth Top Lock. By midday they had reached the summit, and here they paused for lunch before entering the tunnel.

Navigating a boat through a canal tunnel is always a strange experience, but Fawcett seems to have found the passage of Bosworth tunnel singularly unpleasant. Not only was the narrow cavern of crumbling brickwork as cold and dark as a vault after the warmth and brilliance of the May sunshine, but water streamed from the roof and descended in cascades from the chimneys of the ventilation shafts. He had the utmost difficulty in keeping a straight course, for the damp atmosphere exhaled an evil-smelling mist which obscured the farther end of the tunnel and rendered the headlight on the bow ineffective. All he could see ahead was a lambent white curtain, patterned confusingly with shifting shadows. At one moment he thought he saw Charles leaning dangerously over the gunwale at the bow, and called out, fearing he would strike his head against the tunnel wall. But Charles answered from the aft cabin close at hand and the shadow presently vanished.

At length, a wan disc of daylight appeared and they presently emerged from the mists into the bright sunlight of the short pound between the tunnel mouth and Bosworth Top Lock. The canal here is well sheltered by the slopes of Bosworth Wood. On the one hand, the trees grow down to the water's edge, but on the towing-path side a narrow border of smooth, green turf intervenes. It looks an ideal mooring, and Fawcett wondered why the lock-keeper at Canonshanger should have advised him to lie below the lock. Not only did this appear less inviting, but it was farther from the village. His recommendation seemed even less explicable when, having brought the *Wildflower* alongside the bank, Charles discovered rusty mooring rings buried beneath the turf. Obviously it was here that, in the days of horse-drawn traffic, the horses were detached and led over the hill while the boats were laboriously 'legged' through the tunnel. Now the horse-path has become a little-used footway climbing up the wooded slope towards the village, and in places almost blinded by the thick undergrowth of briar and hazel. It was up this path that Charles set forth half an hour later, just in time to catch the afternoon train from that sleepy station called Cold Bosworth and Marborough Road.

Fawcett was too well accustomed to his own company to feel lonely or at a loss after the departure of his friend. When he had brewed himself a pot of tea he filled his pipe, got out his rod, and sat out on the deck fishing. Though he caught nothing he was well content, for the contemplation of his motionless float was little more than an excuse for the enjoyment of a fine evening. The westering sunlight threw golden, moted rays between trees resplendent with new leaf, and the wood was loud with birdsong. The smoke of Fawcett's pipe made a thin, blue column in the windless air. Yet when the sun left the wood and the shadows began to gather around the mouth of the tunnel it grew chilly and he went below. He cooked himself a liberal supper, wrote up the log for the day and then, with a sigh of contentment, turned in to his comfortable bunk. But for some unaccountable reason he was denied his customary sound sleep. After a fitful doze, during which he tossed and turned uneasily, he suddenly awoke to full consciousness, and the dawn was already breaking before he slept again. Two distracting sounds contributed to this wakefulness. One was a soft, recurrent thudding as though some resilient object, floating in the water, occasionally nudged the hull of the boat. The other was a faint but desolate wailing, rising and falling in mournful, irregular cadences and sounding, now close about the boat and now infinitely far off. It seemed to come from the direction of the tunnel, and though Fawcett could see through his cabin window a pattern of branches in motionless silhouette against the moonlight, he concluded it must be some trick of the wind blowing over the top of one of the ventilation shafts. With the aid of a boat-hook he might, he reflected, dispose of one of these disturbances at all events, yet for some reason he felt singularly disinclined to leave his bed. He excused himself upon the grounds that the night seemed to be remarkably cold for the time of the year.

The following day passed uneventfully. After his uncomfortable night, Fawcett slept late and consequently it was nearly noon when, breakfast disposed of, he set off for Cold Bosworth to replenish his stores at the village shop. On his return, he spent the rest of another glorious afternoon happily engaged upon the numerous small jobs which can always be found on a boat. Charles was due to return the following morning, and this was a good opportunity to get everything ship-shape before they continued their journey. Tomorrow there must be no lying late abed, so he turned in early, and this time fell almost immediately into a deep sleep.

Whether what followed was a dream or not must be left for the reader to judge. He suddenly found himself standing on the stern of the *Wildflower* and peering into the mouth of the tunnel. He had no idea why he was doing so or what he expected to see, for though the moon was bright the blackness of the tunnel was impenetrable. The night was calm and beautiful, the moon-silvered water reflecting dark arabesques of leaf and branch with mirror-like perfection. Yet somehow the whole scene seemed to have become charged with that sense of imminent terror which is the prelude of nightmare. Still he continued to stare wide-eyed into the blackness, seeing nothing and hearing only the hollow echoing plash of the water which dripped from the tunnel roof. But at length he perceived a thickening of the shadows beneath the curving abutment wall, and presently saw a figure, more shade than substance, move down to the margin to crouch and stare into the still water. It moved without sound, and only the face showed pale in the moonlight. For a time, the figure seemed to grope beside the water, and Fawcett knew, without knowing why he knew, that it sought for something which it feared to find. Then with a swift movement which suggested that it had been startled by some sound inaudible to Fawcett, the figure rose and turned to peer intently into the tunnel. It was at this moment that the feeling of ominous expectancy, which all this while had been gathering like a thunder-cloud in Fawcett's mind, suddenly assumed most hideous shape. Something rose out of the water; something monstrous that the reason most vehemently questioned, yet which possessed the semblance of human shape. Mercifully, it could not be clearly seen. The face, if face there was, seemed to be hidden by dark hair as by a veil, but the phosphorescence of corruption dimly suggested a nakedness of obscene distension. The dark watcher on the bank, with a gesture of despair, made to turn away, but stumbled. Upon the instant his fearful antagonist fell upon him with such lithe and intent purpose that the issue of the brief and soundless encounter was never in doubt, and soon the waters had closed over them both.

Now long before this, Fawcett should have awakened with a shout to find himself trembling and sweating in his bed. But he maintains that there was no awakening; that his fear gradually ebbed away until he realized that he was in truth shivering in his pyjamas on the aft deck of the *Wildflower*. I have little doubt that the physical and mental rigours of this experience were at least partly responsible for his early death, for there is no further entry in the log, and I conjecture that it was his friend Charles who took the *Wildflower* on to Horton Junction, where she lay until she was sold.

My recollection of Fawcett convinced me that he had experienced something more than a nightmare accompanied by a risky feat of somnambulism, and it was this conviction which took me to Cold Bosworth. I will not weary the reader with all the details of a search which took me from the lock-keeper at Canonshanger, through the dusty files of the *Marborough Messenger*, to the tomb in the churchyard to which I have already referred.

The lock-keeper at Canonshanger proved to be uncommunicative and sceptical, though he admitted that the summit pound east of the tunnel was said by the boatmen to be 'disturbed' and that on this account they would never tie up there.

Old Tom Okey at Bosworth locks, however, was more loquacious. 'They do say,' he vouchsafed, 'that summit be troubled by a chap what drownded hisself there a long time back,' and it was this observation which was really the starting-point of my research.

The story begins, not with 'the chap what drownded hisself', but with Mary Grimsden. She lived with her widowed mother in a small cottage, pulled down many years ago, which stood on common land on the fringe of Canonshanger woods. They appear to have been of gypsy stock, and Rebecca Grimsden is described as a herbalist. From this and other references I gather that she must have been a formidable old woman who, had she lived in an earlier period, might well have suffered death as a witch. It seems that Mary took after her mother, but this did not prevent young John Lofthouse from falling a victim to her dark good looks. The Lofthouses were substantial yeomen farmers who had held Coppice Farm for generations, so that it is easy to understand why the infatuation of their heir with a cottager of doubtful antecedents and dubious occupation soon set tongues wagging. Eventually, news of the affair reached the ears of his family, and the young man, who by this time may have realized the extent of his folly, undertook to see his Mary no more. Yet rumour hinted that the girl was with child by young John and that she intended by this means to retaliate against her faithless lover and his family. But from this embarrassing eventuality the family of Lofthouse were spared by an unforeseen and surprising circumstance. At dusk on a fine evening in the August of 1840, Mary Grimsden walked out of the little cottage at Canonshanger and never returned. Despite a most extensive search, no trace of her could be found, and though he had forsworn her, it was remarked that John Lofthouse appeared to be deeply affected by her loss. Though old Rebecca Grimsden persisted that she had been the victim of foul play, the village seems to have come to the conclusion that Mary's gypsy blood had got the better of her.

Hardly had the talk aroused by this affair died down when, in February of the following year, on the night of the fourteenth to be exact, it found fresh and startling matter in the disappearance of John Lofthouse. But this time the mystery was soon solved. A local boatman, who had delivered a cargo of lime for Coppice Farm and was working late down the Bosworth locks, claimed to have seen on the tow-path the figure of 'young mister John' walking swiftly and alone in the direction of the tunnel. Acting upon the strength of this evidence, it was decided to drag the canal beginning at the east portal of the tunnel. This led, almost immediately, to a discovery of a most shocking nature. For not only was the body of John Lofthouse recovered, but entangled within the grappling irons was another. Because the latter had been long dead, it was unrecognizable, nor was it possible to determine the cause of death. Death in such a form is never pleasant to behold, but this discovery seems to have had a singularly disconcerting effect upon the beholders.

Though the canal had been dragged without result at the time of Mary's disappearance, Rebecca Grimsden identified a ring recovered with the body as having belonged to her daughter. Had it not subsequently been confirmed by other more reliable witnesses, it is doubtful if this evidence of identification would have been admissible for, to judge from her conduct at the inquest, the old woman was out of her mind. Usually grim enough, there is a peculiar quality of the macabre about the account of the proceedings at this inquest. In the first place, when ordered to view the bodies of the deceased, the jury were so affected that proceedings had to be suspended for a time. When the hearing was eventually resumed, Rebecca Grimsden's interruptions made matters worse, for she seemed to be labouring under the ghastly illusion that she was attending her daughter's nuptials. Together with other singular observations, which are not recorded, she kept reiterating that she had fulfilled her promise to provide her daughter with a bridegroom, an assertion which proved to be so disquieting that the coroner was compelled to order her removal from the court.

Despite evidence that John Lofthouse had become increasingly morose since Mary Grimsden's disappearance, an open verdict was returned in both cases, perhaps in deference to the feelings of the young man's family. Yet why that family should have consented to the burial of their son in a common grave with a gypsy girl, and why they caused to be erected over it so curious a memorial is not explained. I have formed my own conclusion which I prefer not to discuss.

While we shall never know what occurred on that sultry August night so long ago when Mary Grimsden disappeared, I may mention in conclusion a discovery of my own which I consider significant. I was exploring the wood which gives Coppice Farm its name when I came across a circular wall of old brickwork, and, upon investigation, found that it protected the mouth of one of the ventilation shafts of Bosworth tunnel. The wall was not so high that an active man might not thereby rid himself of a heavy and unwelcome burden, and as I leant over the parapet I could hear, as from a well, the drip of water far below.

I returned in the gathering dusk of that winter evening past the east portal of the tunnel and along the towing-path. The water looked black and was very still under the shadow of the trees. Though I would assure the reader that I am not a credulous man, I have to admit that I felt disinclined to stop and look about me, but hurried on, keeping as far as possible from the water's edge, and must confess to a feeling of profound relief when I reached the lower level below the top lock.

NEW CORNER

The Blighs were late as usual, and practice day was nearly over when their familiar old Vauxhall with its loaded trailer rumbled into the paddock.

It was the first meeting of the 1938 season at the famous Highbury Hill, and promised to be the best of a long series, for the enthusiastic organizers, the Mercia Motor Club, had been preparing for the event as never before. Not only had they managed to secure an international date for the first time, but they had improved the hill out of all recognition, widening, re-surfacing and constructing one entirely new section of road. These efforts had been justly rewarded by what was probably the finest entry list that a speed hill climb in this country had ever produced.

Germany had sent over one of her Grand Prix Rheinwagens – a 3-litre, 16-cylinder, rear-engined job – to be handled by no less a person than Von Eberstraum himself. France had entered her most successful driver, Camille, with Monsieur Rene Lefevre's latest masterpiece, a double-cam straight-eight of conventional design – somewhat untried, but a joy to the eye, like all Rene's cars. Most noteworthy of all, Italy was to be represented by her veteran 'Maestro', Emilio Volanti, driving a marque which had not been associated with his name for some time, a 3-litre Maturati, the first Italian car seriously to challenge German speed supremacy.

The British reply to this formidable Continental opposition was provided by the works team of B.R.C.'s, and a host of sprint 'specials'. The former were smaller than their Continental rivals, but the course suited them and, with the exception of the new section, their drivers had the advantage of knowing the hill intimately.

The 'specials' were, as always, an unknown quantity. Some, on their day, were quite capable of matching the performance of the Grand Prix cars over such a short course, while others might merely provide comic relief by emitting remarkably irregular noises and bestrewing the course with intimate parts of their machinery.

There was no doubt about it, the stage was set for a record meeting. No wonder Mr Nelson, the genial little secretary and moving spirit of the M.M.C., had felt excited and pleased with himself that morning when he had watched lorries bearing names famous on all the circuits of Europe come rolling into his paddock.

Brothers Peter and John lost no time in unloading the Bligh Special from its trailer.

'If you go and rout out the Scrutineer,' said Peter, as they man-handled the Special into its bay, 'I'll go and talk nicely to Nelson and see if I can't wangle one run before dark.'

John had barely finished unloading from the tonneau of the Vauxhall the cans of dope, the tools and all the other paraphernalia that accompanies the sprint car, when Peter came back at the double.

'It's Okay,' he called. 'But we shall have to hurry; Nelson's sending over the Scrutineer. Meantime, we've got to go for a walk, blast it! All drivers have got to go over the new section on foot and report to the timing-box that they've done so before they're allowed a run.' He paused, peering round the paddock. 'I wonder where those silly asses can have got to? I told them to keep a look out for us,' he complained.

'Maybe they've got fed up with waiting and gone off to the "Crown",' John hazarded.

'I'll half break their silly necks if they have,' Peter swore. 'No, there they are snooping around the Maturati. Oi!' he bellowed. 'Mike! George!'

Two tall, untidy figures detached themselves from the curious group about the Italian car and came towards them at a jog-trot.

'Where the hell have you been?' shouted one as soon as he came within earshot. 'We'd just given you up – thought you must have thrown the trailer away again on the way, so we were just going to make for the local tap-house.'

'Never mind about that now,' Peter silenced him. 'Your thirst will improve with keeping. The great thing at the moment is to get a practice run before dark. John and I have got to walk over the new bit of the course, so if you'd like to make yourself really useful for a change, you can get her ready and warmed up while we're away. That's the dope-can, the one with the white top. It's all ready mixed. The soft plugs are in, but you'd better have a look at them before you try a start. When she's just about sizzling, put in the R2's, they're in that yellow box. Oh, and another thing,' he added, 'the Scrutineer is on his way, so none of your rudery or he may take a poor view of John's idea of independent suspension,'

'As you say, Chief,' Mike replied with mock humility, and pulled his forelock. Yet he took his coat off and set to work with a will, ably assisted by the quiet George, while the others set off up the course.

Whereas the old road wound its way up through the wood in a series of zigzag curves, thus gaining height on an easy gradient, the new section left the old at the first of these corners, and cut straight and steeply up the hill-side for a distance of 300 yards to a single left-hand turn. This was followed by another straight on a slightly easier gradient, which ran parallel with the flank of the hill until it rejoined the old course, at what had previously been the very slow Creek Hairpin.

Peter and John stood on the apex of the new corner, surveying it with critical and practised eyes.

'There's no doubt about it, this is a great improvement,' John decided. 'It'll make the course much faster and more interesting, too. This "swerve" reminds me of the first bend of the "esse" at Shelsley; same gradient up to it, I should think, same curvature and camber, and the same bank on the outside, too, for the unwary to clout.'

'Of course, it's difficult to judge just how steep that approach is, so that one can't tell exactly where the cut-off point will be, but I should say it will be just about opposite those stones there.'

He pointed out two great boulders that stood like monoliths, one on each side of the road. Peter nodded.

'I think you're right,' he agreed. 'It looks straightforward enough and yet – oh, I don't know – there's something I don't like about it, but exactly what it is I couldn't tell you. Phew!' he exclaimed and laughed shortly, 'what a stink! Old socks and rotten eggs aren't in it. Something must have died here a long time ago I should think.'

'That's funny,' said John, sniffing. 'I don't notice it. Anyway, we'd better get down, it seems to be getting dark all of a sudden under these trees, so unless we hurry we shan't have enough light for a run.'

When they got back to the paddock practically everyone had packed up for the night, but the faithful Mike and his shadow George had the Special ready and only awaiting a push to the line. Peter wriggled his way into the narrow bucket-seat in front of the two potent 'Vee' twin engines and the others pushed.

Letting in the clutch, he was greeted with the deafening staccato bark of four open exhausts belching blue flame and a reek of dope and castor-oil. For a few moments the air about the timing-box was filled with an intensity of urgent sound that literally stung the ear-drums to painful protest, while Peter tightened his body-belt, pulled down his goggles and exchanged a last shouted word or two with John.

Then at a nodded signal Mike released the plungers of the two oil-pumps and stepped back, the note of the engines rose even more fiercely, and the next instant the car was snaking out of sight in a series of power slides, leaving in its wake two long, black streaks of pungent burnt rubber from the tyres.

'A bit too much loud pedal there,' Mike commented.

Although invisible to him, John could follow Peter's progress by the noise that now resounded through the wood and echoed about the surrounding hills. Now he had cut-out and changed down for the first corner into the wood – a sharp one that – now he was round and accelerating away for all he was worth up the steep straight to the new corner; he was through to second, now into third – that was a surprise, he had not expected that Peter would get into third. Now he had cut-out for the new corner.

John waited expectantly for a renewed burst of sound, but no sound came. He must have crashed. Then, after what seemed an age of suspense, but must in reality have been but a second or two, he heard the sound of one engine come to life and continue over the top of the hill. John heaved a sigh of relief and walked round to meet the car at the foot of the return road; anyway, Peter and the Special were still in one piece.

Peter came coasting back in a fine fury, consigning with great fluency the M.M.C., the hill, the local inhabitants, and the new corner to a particularly lurid hell. John gave him a few moments in which to simmer down before he dared to enquire what had happened.

'What happened?' Peter exploded with renewed fury. 'Well, I was going a treat, as you probably heard. Pulling third on the straight, too, when just as I came into the new corner some suicidal idiot came flapping out at me waving his arms plumb in the middle of the road. It meant that I had to brake and alter course right in the middle of the corner, and it was no fault of his that I didn't pile up the whole outfit. As it was, I just touched the bank on the outside, shot across the road, went up on the grass on the inside and eventually managed to get back on to the road again. By that time one engine had cut out; still, I think the car's all right. We shall have to get up bright and early and get in a couple of runs tomorrow morning, that's all, there's not enough light in the wood for another run now.'

When the Blighs eventually arrived at the 'Crown' in Winchford where they had arranged to stay, they found Mr Nelson leaning on the bar, chatting to Camille and Butt, the number one B.R.C. driver. He looked up and smiled as they came in.

'Well, how did you get on, Bligh?' he enquired.

Peter grinned ruefully.

'Oh, all right, thanks, as far as it went, which wasn't very far, I'm afraid.'

'You're not going to tell me you had trouble on the new corner, are you?' Mr Nelson implored. 'Everyone seems to have been in difficulties there. I've heard nothing but complaints about it all day. The surface, the camber, the light – nothing seems to be right about it. It's pretty disheartening for me after so much work. Even Volanti said he had a nasty moment there, although he put up an excellent time. Three people have hit the bank, fortunately without serious damage, and several others had their engines die quite unaccountably when they came to open up after the corner.' Mr Nelson looked quite downcast.

'Oh, no,' Peter hastened to assure him. 'I've got no complaint to make against the corner itself, but just as I came into it some fool popped out from nowhere right into the middle of the road, waving his arms like a lunatic. Result was, I had a very busy time indeed, and while I was motoring about on the grass and dodging trees I lost one engine.'

Poor conscientious Mr Nelson looked more harassed than ever and swore under his breath.

'I'm most frightfully sorry to hear about this, Bligh,' he apologized. 'I can't think who can have done such a crazy thing. When you went up, the marshals had just come down and reported to me that there were no spectators left on the hill, and only Arthur Day was still up there, hanging on in the top timing-box until you had made your run. Tell me, what did this idiot look like?'

Peter thought for a moment before replying.

'Well,' he explained, 'the light was pretty poor under the trees there by the time I went up, and anyway you can't notice much detail when you're "dicing", but he seemed a tall, thin bloke wearing something white. It looked like an overall coat, or it may have been a very light-coloured mackintosh.

'The odd thing that struck me, now I come to think of it, was that he didn't seem to have the coat on properly – his arms through the sleeves I mean – but slung round his shoulders, so that it looked like – well – more like a surplice than anything else.'

He laughed.

'I'm not trying to suggest, though, that it may have been the local padre in his war-paint or anything like that. Just as I got the car back on to the road,' he went on, 'I had a quick look round, but he must have made a lightning getaway, for I couldn't see a sign of him. Anyway,' Peter concluded, 'I'm not worrying, it was my own fault for turning up so late. What'll you have to drink?' he asked.

The conversation became general and the usual topics that are raised on the eve of a speed event were discussed at length. Talk was of blowers and blower pressures, of gear ratios, suspension and braking systems and of twin rear wheels versus single.

Mr Nelson played his part nobly in this discussion, for he was secretly a prey to a vague feeling of uneasiness, a dim sense of foreboding, which began to get the upper hand later, when he found himself alone in his room for the night. That confounded new corner seemed to be at the bottom of everything, he reflected; what an unlucky job it had been from start to finish! A constant worry. At one time he had seriously doubted whether the road would ever be ready in time, they had had such a long chapter of accidents and irritating annoyances.

In the first place, the local wiseacres had been even more pig-headed and obstinate than usual, and had not only refused to help the work of the club in any way, but had actually seemed bent on putting obstacles in their path. None of the local contractors could be persuaded to take on the job, and he had been compelled to employ a London firm at much greater expense. All this because of some archaic superstition about a ring of old stones through which the road would pass.

To begin with, some foolish practical joker, presumably one of the villagers, kept moving the surveyor's pegs and sights overnight, and once they had even been collected together and burnt. Next, a large oak-tree they were felling, thanks to an unexpected and violent gust of wind on an otherwise calm day, fell unexpectedly in the wrong direction. It trapped the foreman, seriously injuring him, while several of the men had narrow escapes.

The mechanical navvy broke down repeatedly, until finally a subsidence occurred beneath it, and it required days of digging and the erection of shear-legs before it could be extricated. Just when the excavations were nearly at an end, and they were preparing to lay the foundations of the road, a spring had been struck, which made the whole hillside a hopeless quagmire of mud.

Then the trouble began among the workmen. Several of them fell victims to a peculiar and singularly unpleasant complaint, from which two had subsequently died, and the remainder had become restless and uneasy, saying there was no luck on the job. No doubt local talk was responsible.

Seeing the work was so behind time, he had tried to persuade the contractor to put on a night shift, offering to provide them with flares, but the men had resolutely refused to work after sundown. It was only by the dogged persistence of Mr Nelson himself that the road had been completed in time for the event, and it was with a sense of personal triumph that he had opened the course to competitors.

When beset by all these difficulties, he had actually begun to wonder at times whether there might not, after all, be some truth in local superstitions, but when the new road was at last finished and he toured up it at the wheel of his blue saloon Le Fevre, this disturbing thought had been forgotten. Now, the unfortunate mishaps in practice and particularly Bligh's story had recalled his past uneasiness.

He recollected how he had dismissed impatiently the workmen's talk of something or someone flitting about among the trees; never seen in broad daylight, but only after sundown, often glimpsed in the corner of the eye, but never directly seen. Strange, too, that both workmen and drivers had complained of the unpleasant stench that occasionally seemed to hang about the corner.

In an attempt to put a stop to these disquieting and unprofitable thoughts, Mr Nelson decided to indulge in his favourite relaxation of reading in bed. After a while the book slipped from his hand on to the coverlet and he fell into an uneasy sleep, which brought with it a very vivid and disturbing dream.

He was sitting in his favourite position in the lower timing-box at Longbury. It was evidently late in the day, for the light seemed subdued. Through the window he could see the Rheinwagen on the starting-line with Von Eberstraum at the wheel. For no apparent reason this perfectly normal spectacle seemed to inspire him with dreadful uneasiness. He felt as though he was the unwilling witness of some sinister sequence of events which he was quite powerless to interrupt.

He saw the starter place the contact shoe before the front wheel of the car, and as he did so a voice said quite clearly and distinctly:

'He's out for blood.'

Then the Rheinwagen made its anticipated meteoric get-away. Mr Nelson realized that he had the head-phones on, and he listened anxiously for the reassuring voice of Arthur Day to announce the time. It did not come.

Instead his head became filled with a distant but penetrating reverberation of sound. It was like nothing he had ever heard before, but it most closely resembled the far-off booming of a great gong. Then a thin, high voice began to intone in a tongue that was unintelligible, and yet somehow indescribably menacing. Finally, and seemingly much nearer at hand, someone screamed.

At this point Mr Nelson awoke with the scream still ringing in his ears, to find himself bathed in perspiration, despite the fact that he had kicked most of the bedclothes on to the floor. Disinclined to court further sleep that night, and feeling wretchedly ill at ease, he propped himself upright with his pillows and resigned himself to read his novel, with as much concentration as he could muster, for the rest of the night.

A brilliant spring morning without a cloud in the sky did much to dispel Mr Nelson's gloomy fears and to make amends for his wretched night. He felt inclined to attribute his nightmare to over-indulgence in the 'Crown's' excellent Stilton at dinner the previous evening.

When he opened the course at noon, accompanied by the President of the Club and a minor Royalty, he felt in excellent humour once more. A record crowd of spectators thronged the banks and enclosures on the hill and the fields below were black with cars.

In the interval between the first and second runs Mr Nelson felt justified in laughing at his forebodings, for the unfortunate incidents of practice day had not re-occurred, and the programme had been run off like clockwork. It was obvious that the honour of fastest time of the day lay between Von Eberstraum and Volanti with the Maturati. Von

Eberstraum, it appeared, had a slightly faster car, but he held an advantage of a mere fifth of a second over Volanti, who was handling his car with that almost fabulous skill for which he was justly famous.

A brilliantly judged climb by Butt in No. I B.R.C. won him first place in the 1½-litre class, and third in the general classification, while the Bligh Special had made an ear-splitting run to record the fastest time by a sprint 'special'. The performance of the new Lefevre was a little disappointing, and Camille could only manage fifth place. Mr Nelson could see him in the paddock now, explaining volubly and with a wealth of gesture typically Gallic, to a group of equally vociferous mechanics, why the car was quite useless and unfit for him, the great Camille, to drive.

It was just as the first car was being brought to the line for its second run that an unfortunate and most unusual mishap occurred to delay the proceedings. Without any warning a section of the bank above the new corner gave way and slid down into the road, carrying several spectators with it. Fortunately no one was injured, and amidst much laughter and jesting a gang of amateur navvies was hastily recruited, and set to work with a will to clear the earth on to the inside of the corner. Even so, the delay caused was such that Mr Nelson realized that unless the rest of the programme was run off extremely promptly, the light would fail the last cars.

However, once the obstruction had been cleared and the spectators moved back as a precautionary measure, the second runs were made amidst much excitement, but again without untoward incident. Von Eberstraum and Volanti both made faster, but this time identical times, and sent a message to the timing-box requesting that they be allowed an additional run each to decide the tie. This was granted, though the two drivers were urged to come to the line as soon as possible on account of failing light. The announcement that the tie was about to be run off provoked a murmur of excited anticipation and speculation from the dense crowds on the hill.

Volanti appeared first, as the Rheinwagen mechanics were changing rear wheels. As he was pushed to the line and the engine of the Maturati was started the sun was just sinking beyond the horizon of the vale, and already the outlines of the woods and of the farther hills were becoming indistinct in a blue evening haze.

The 'Maestro' went off like a bullet, his hatchet face set in the determined way that meant business. His time came through surprisingly quickly, Arthur Day's usually quiet voice raised with excitement. It was two-fifths of a second better than his previous run.

Now Von Eberstraum! The silver Rheinwagen was pushed up to the line by the impassive German mechanics. The driver climbed into the cockpit. One mechanic fixed the detachable steering-wheel in place, while another inserted the starting-handle in the tail. At a signal from the driver he gave one sharp flick of the wrist and the engine broke into its characteristic deep-throated roar, little puffs of black smoke spurting vertically upward from sixteen short pipes as the throttle was 'blipped'. Von Eberstraum looked grimly determined as he drew on his gloves and adjusted his goggles. A marshal bent towards Mr Nelson in the timing-box.

'He's out for blood,' he shouted above the roar.

Mr Nelson's heart sank within him, for in a moment he realized that his nightmare of the previous night was being re-enacted before his eyes. Every detail was horribly familiar; the particular quality of the light which seemed to have suddenly become dim; a little unimportant gesture which the starter made as he acknowledged the nod from the timing-box and placed the contact shoe before the wheel.

Once more a sense of inevitably impending tragedy made him feel powerless, but mastering it, he got to his feet and hammered on the glass of the window to the consternation of his colleagues.

'Stop!' he called despairingly. 'Stop him!'

Too late; the words were scarcely out of his mouth when the Rheinwagen left the line with smoking tyres and rocketed away in one terrific, sustained burst of acceleration.

Mr Nelson knew then that what he was about to hear through the head-phones would not be the familiar voice of Arthur Day. He was right.

People started to run and the ambulance dashed up the course. Mercifully, perhaps, Mr Nelson did not see them; he had fainted.

The tragic duel between Volanti and Von Eberstraum was almost the sole topic of discussion in motor-racing circles for months afterwards. As usual, theories as to the cause of the disaster were legion. On only one point were the theorists unanimous. The new corner was in some obscure way highly dangerous.

First Volanti had approached the corner at a fantastic speed, crammed on his brakes, and got into a terrifying and inexplicable slide as though the road had suddenly become a sheet of ice. To the horrified spectators it looked as though a crash was inevitable, and only Volanti's uncanny skill and presence of mind can have saved him. The little man's elbows worked like flails as he fought for control. Instead of the head-on impact which seemed so inevitable, the Maturati caught the bank a glancing blow as the tail swung wide, then rocketed across to the inside as though it must surely plunge over the bank to disaster, but was corrected and held on the very brink, all in a moment of time. Finally, and before the astounded spectators had time to draw breath, the car was on the road again, the howl of the blower burst forth once more like a triumphant cry, and Volanti was gone in a flurry of turf, dust and smoke to set up his incredible record.

A marshal walked up and examined the road surface, suspecting oil, but there was none visible. Many spectators were then driven away from the corner by an appalling stench which suddenly arose. Others, oddly enough, failed to notice it.

Then came Von Eberstraum. The Rheinwagen appeared to be travelling equally rapidly, but seemed quite steady under the terrific braking, and was taking the corner very fast, but apparently under perfect control, when once more the inexplicable happened. In the middle of the corner Von Eberstraum braked suddenly and appeared to alter course, with the result that the car was completely out of control, spun round, and disappeared backwards over the bank on the inside. There was a sickening crashing and splintering as the car bounded over and over through the undergrowth until it eventually came to rest, a mangled wreck, against a great upright block of stone.

The most popular theory of the accident was that the brakes seized, the arm-chair theorists talking glibly of the fluid boiling in the brake pipes as a result of the heavy braking immediately before the corner. They ignored the fact that the braking system fitted to the car had undergone many far more gruelling tests in Grand Prix races.

There were other witnesses of the disaster who had their own shadowy inkling of the possible cause, but preferred to keep it to themselves, because they doubted the evidence of their eyes, having seen what many had apparently failed to see. As Von Eberstraum came into the corner they had fancied that something darted out from the shadow of the bank below them into the path of the car. It was only a fleeting glimpse seen out of the corners of eyes intently focused on the car alone. After the car had gone the road was deserted.

Peter Bligh was amongst those who had vague but disturbing ideas about the accident, which he decided to keep to himself.

Mr Nelson was the only person who was not in the slightest doubt as to the cause, although he, too, preferred to keep his own counsel. His first action after his recovery from a severe nervous breakdown was to order a high and unclimbable fence to be erected all round the new corner.

Some of you may have wondered, like I did, why such a promising and costly improvement of Longbury Hill should be allowed to fall into disuse so soon. I have at last managed to get the real facts from Mr Nelson and Peter Bligh. So now you know, and may draw your own conclusions. Personally, I agree with Mr Nelson. I think there is something on the inside of that fence that is best left alone.

CWM GARON

After a long winter spent in the fog and grime of London, this Welsh Borderland was balm to the eye. Spring had only just touched the soot-blackened trees in the squares with the lightest film of green, but here she had already run riot, dressing the whole countryside in fresh splendour. So thought John Carfax as the labouring branch-line train bore him slowly over the last stage of his long journey to Wales. The map lay disregarded on his knees as he watched the moving panorama of hills stippled with April cloud shadows, of neat farms buried in the white mist of fruit orchards, and of rich meadows dotted with sheep or the red cattle of Herefordshire. He was in that mood of exhilaration and heightened perception which only a well-earned and long-awaited holiday in new surroundings can awaken, and he sniffed delightedly at the limpid air, crystaline as spring water yet somehow filled with unidentifiable sweetness, which blew in through the open window. He was alone in the compartment now, but it had evidently been market day in the town where he had left the London express, for the little train standing at the bay platform had been filled with country folk. Black-gaitered farmers and their plump, basket-laden wives, all had gone, but still he seemed to smell sheep-dip and carbolic, to hear the lilt of their Border speech, and to see the lithe Welsh sheep-dog which had sat between his master's legs, regarding him with wall-eyed suspicion.

The rhythm of wheels over rail joints slowed, and Carfax could tell from the labouring exhaust beats of the engine that they were climbing steeply. A chasm-like cutting hewn through the old red sandstone cut off the view and plunged the compartment into sudden twilight. As suddenly, the train emerged and, with a hollow reverberation, crossed a swift mountain torrent, before swinging round a curve so sharp that the wheel flanges grunted and squealed in protest. As it did so, the carriage window framed a picture which made Carfax start and catch his breath in wonder, so startling was it in its wild grandeur after looking so long on the smooth fields and hills of England. A towering mountain wall had suddenly arisen to enclose the whole western horizon, and to dominate and dwarf the familiar landscape of the foreground. Seen thus against the westering light of late afternoon, the shadowed face of this great massif presented so marked a contrast to the sunlit levels below as to seem unreal and as menacing as a thunder-cloud. So impenetrable was the shadow on the mountain that its contours were invisible, and the long, level line of the ridge, sharply etched across the sky's brightness, appeared to mark the lip of a precipice the height of which seemed monstrously magnified.

Reluctantly, John Carfax turned his attention from the window to the map. Then, as he felt the brakes applied, he got up and lifted his rucksack down from the luggage rack. This must be Pont Newydd; he would have to step out if he was to cross the mountain and reach the inn at Llangaron Abbey by nightfall. A good map-reader, he had no doubt of his ability to find his way through strange country by daylight, but to be overtaken by darkness on an open mountain was a very different matter. He welcomed the prospect of the long, hard walk after the inactivity of the train journey, and set off at a smart pace up the narrow road from the station. Behind him, he heard the train pant heavily out of earshot. It seemed to symbolize the last link between him and the civilization he had so lately left, and as he turned to glance at the thin plume of steam fast vanishing into the distance he felt something of the sensation a voyager feels when, landed on some remote, far distant island, he sees the ship that has brought him fade over the horizon. He experienced momentarily a strange feeling of loneliness, realizing that the train was an intruder from that world of elaborate artifice by means of which man had shut himself away from the eternal world of earth and sky as though fearful of their elemental mystery. It had ruffled a still pool of silence, but now the last ripples died away into stillness, until there remained no sounds but his own footfall, a distant rumour of birdsong and the sibillant voice of the little brook which ran beside the road.

He had been walking for the best part of an hour before he came in sight of the first of the landmarks he had previously noted on his map, a grey, ruined tower set upon a conical mound and surrounded by a ditch. He conjectured correctly that it was one of the border keeps erected by the Norman Lords Marcher in their efforts to subdue the Silurians of the mountains. Here, turning off the metalled road into a rutted, high-banked lane, he set his face towards the mountain wall which had hitherto marched on his left hand. Pressing on, he passed by two small white-washed farms where sheep-dogs ran out to bark and sniff at his heels, but though the lane climbed continuously, the skyline of the ridge seemed to retreat elusively before him. At length, however, he emerged on to a level plateau, treeless except for a few stunted thorn bushes, and patterned by crumbling, dry stone walls which had proved powerless to resist the downward march of the bracken. Here he came within the mountain's shadow, so that his eyes could, for the first time, penetrate its darkness to discern the steep diagonal path which scaled the ridge. Following its upward course he could see, too, the shallow notch cut in the skyline of the ridge which marked the pass, if 'pass' it could be called, for his map told him that the path climbed almost to the 2000 feet contour. The premature dusk of the shadow spurred him on, and he had soon passed through a rickety gate on to the open mountain and was tackling the steep ascent. Pausing on the break-neck path to regain his breath, he turned and saw that already the plateau, which had seemed so high and windswept, now looked insignificant, merging imperceptibly into a vast chequer-work of field and copse whose folds this height had now smoothed out. He plodded on, and had nearly reached the summit before he stopped and turned again to find that the familiar landscape had shrunk to a remote perspective, while the evening sunlight on the farther fields looked pallid and unreal as though seen through a veil. Glancing about him he saw the reason. A white wall of cloud was rolling along the ridge out of the north-west, and in the next instant the scene below was lost in swirling mist. No rain fell, but his rough tweed jacket was soon pearled with beads of moisture, while a chill wind blew about him.

The sudden coming of the mist brought with it a feeling of utter isolation, intensifying the loneliness he had felt when he left the station. It seemed to mark a further stage in some inexorable progress designed deliberately to cut him off from the familiar world of his fellow-men. Sole occupant of a minute island of mountain turf, heather and whinberry, that familiar world already seemed incredibly remote. Fortunately for him, the path was clearly defined, so that he was able to press on without pause or doubt. And as he did so, some curious trick of the silver light threw his shadow upon the white curtain before him so that it seemed that a figure, monstrous, yet tenuous as the mist itself, was leading him onward towards the summit of the pass. Watching it, he thought he could understand the stories he had heard of the creatures which were believed to haunt the mountain mists, and he felt he knew the terror that might come with this loneliness as terror comes with darkness to the child. His heart seemed to beat in his ears like a muffled drum, for the stillness was intent, even his footfall was muffled now by the resilient turf of the path. When, faint and far off, his ear caught the cry of a curlew, the sound brought no comforting sense of companionship, but by its plaintive wildness, seemed only to accentuate the silence and the loneliness. Suddenly, the path swung right-handed, levelled out, and he found himself passing through a narrow defile which he knew must mark the spine of the ridge. Immediately beyond the pass, the track skirted a mawne pit, a hole from which peats had once been dug, but which had now become a quagmire ringed by livid green moss and tufted cotton-grass. A luckless mountain pony had evidently floundered into it at some time and, unable to extricate itself, had perished miserably. Now that ravens, crows and mountain foxes had done their work, all that remained was a skeleton of whitened bones wrapped in the hide as in a winding-sheet. Carfax paused for a moment at this desolate sight, and as he did so the curlew cried again, nearer at hand this time, and the mist seemed to eddy more densely about him. He shivered involuntarily and went on, happy to find that the path was now leading him downwards as steeply as it had climbed. As he stumbled along, his feet pressing uncomfortably into the toes of his shoes, he noticed that the mist was now thinning, and that its whiteness was becoming suffused with golden light although the invisible depths into which he was descending still seemed dark. Not only was he walking out of the mists, but the cloud itself appeared to be lifting, sweeping up the steep flank of the mountain like steam out of a cauldron until, with breath-taking and dramatic suddenness, the veil which had imprisoned and blinded him lifted like a curtain to reveal the whole wild prospect clearly before him. 'You'll find the valley enchanting' – he suddenly recalled the words of the friend who had first suggested his holiday, not in their original sense as a conventional overstatement, but with a new, and strangely literal significance.

He stood in the last stormy light of a sun that was just about to set behind the rim of yet another mountain ridge which marched parallel with that upon which he stood, and which appeared to be of equal, if not greater height. It could not be much more than a mile by crow-flight, he judged, from ridge to ridge, yet between them yawned Cwm Garon, a stupendous furrow which, in the course of unnumbered centuries, the Afon Garon had carved into the heart of the mountains. Already this valley was wrapped in the blue shades of a premature twilight, yet Carfax could sense rather than see the intense green of the meadows along the floor of the Cwm. Here and there, lights gleamed from farmhouse windows. Faintly there rose into the thin mountain air the resinous incense of pine-wood smoke, and the murmur of the swiftly flowing river. At one point the valley widened into a natural amphitheatre in the centre of which stood the grey shape of a building larger than a mountain farm. This Carfax took to be his destination, the ruined Abbey of Llangaron and its adjoining inn. After the cloud-blinded solitude of the mountain-top, the sight of his goal raised his spirits to high good humour, and he strode on down the steep path at a great pace, his mind occupied with the prospect of a blazing fire, a well-earned dinner and a foaming tankard.

Great anticipations are often the prelude to disillusionment, but in this instance John Carfax was not disappointed. The dinner was excellent, and he gave a sigh of contentment as he stirred his coffee and extended his slippered feet towards the friendly flame of the logfire. Its warmth was welcome for the spring nights were chilly in this valley which the sun so soon forsook. In the opposite chimney-corner, likewise toasting his toes, sat his only fellow-guest at the inn. He was busily writing in what appeared to Carfax to be a large journal or diary which he balanced on his knee, and the tireless scratching of his pen mingled with the comfortable crackling of the fire, and the occasional faint bubbling sound which Carfax's pipe made when he drew deeply. In London, he thought, it is never truly quiet, but here one becomes conscious of the slightest sound. He had exhcanged generalities with his companion during their meal when they had sat together, but the latter had not been very forthcoming. He was much older than Carfax; in middle age he had obviously been a man of great strength, tall and broad in proportion. Now the wide shoulders stooped, and a suit of rough, grey tweed hung loosely about his gaunt frame. Yet it was obvious that he was still very active, nor had his presence lost its power of command. A fine head of white hair and a short, pointed beard meticulously trimmed made a fitting frame for the massive brow and the distinguished features. The most remarkable thing about these features, Carfax thought, were the eyes, bright blue eyes which had no need of glasses and whose keenness quite belied his age. When he had spoken he had regarded his fellow-guest with a penetrating, unblinking gaze that was almost hypnotic in its intensity and which, in a lesser man, would have seemed mere ill-mannered arrogance. Carfax found it disconcerting, for it gave him the impression that a keen intelligence, possessing a store of secret knowledge, was coolly taking the measure of his own mind while it remained itself inscrutable, permitting him no such liberty. He recalled with a slight feeling of resentment that whereas he had straightway introduced himself, the other had not responded similarly.

He yawned and must have dozed, for he suddenly became conscious that the fire had burned lower, and that the bole of his pipe was cold. He hoped that he had not snored, and glanced apprehensively at his companion. If he had, it would seem that his manners had passed unnoticed for the other's head was still bent over his book and his pen travelled imperturbably on. He glanced at his watch. The hour was not late, but the long journey, the keen air and the warmth of the fire had told upon him, and his eyelids were heavy with sleep. He rose to go to bed, but before doing so some chance impulse made him walk to the window, part the curtains and look out.

The night was clear, and a bright moon, near the full, rode above a wrack of clouds which was drifting like smoke from lip to lip of the defile. Yet despite the swiftly moving clouds overhead an absolute stillness held the valley, for the trees stood motionless. Only the unseen river, rushing over its rocky bed, sounded incessantly. The window looked directly up the roofless nave of the Abbey, and the great columns threw upon the moonlit grass, shadows so dense that the eye could scarcely distinguish image from substance. Beyond, above the site of the high altar, the great east window, devoid of tracery, framed the dark brooding shape of the mountain which Carfax had crossed that evening. The scene was so extravagant in its chiaroscuro, so humiliating in its grandeur, that he could not restrain a muttered exclamation –

> 'Oh who will tell me where
> He found thee at that dead and silent hour?
> What hallowed solitary ground did bear
>   So rare a flower
> Within whose sacred leaves did lie
> The fullness of the Deity?'

It was appropriate that these lines of the Silurist should have sprung to his mind, for it was not surprising, he reflected, that this country should have been the inspiration of Vaughan and Traherne. Here, truly, heaven seemed nearer earth . . .

'And hell, too, maybe.'

Carfax started, not only because the voice sounded close at his elbow, but because he was not aware that he had spoken his thoughts aloud. He realized that his taciturn companion had moved silently from his chair and was gazing out into the night with those strange, unblinking eyes of his.

'Yes,' he went on in a soft, ruminative tone, as though he were speaking more to himself than to Carfax, 'it is certainly very beautiful, so beautiful that it distils some influence – call it magic if you like – which turns men's minds from material to spiritual things. Unless I am much mistaken, it set you thinking of the Dominicans who built their great church in this solitude, and of the Silurists, Traherne and Vaughan.'

Carfax turned back into the room, letting the curtain fall across the window. The uncanny accuracy with which the other had read his thoughts disturbed him.

His expression must have revealed this disquiet, for the other chuckled. 'I must really apologize,' he went on, 'if I startled you. I can assure you I am not really such an accomplished thought-reader. Let me explain: I have visited this valley on numerous occasions spread over a period of years, and I know that on first acquaintance it always casts this same spell over visitors who, like yourself, are gifted with imagination. All I have done was to observe in you the familiar symptoms.'

Carfax was somewhat mollified, though he still felt slightly irritated by the other's self-assurance, and by the way in which he talked of what had been to him a profound spiritual experience as though it were a cold in the head. Nevertheless, his companion's words had roused his curiosity.

'What exactly do you mean by saying "on first acquaintance"?' he asked. 'Are you suggesting that my present impression of Cwm Garon is likely to change? And what did you mean by your odd remark about hell?'

'Taking the first question first,' replied the other, 'if I have judged you correctly, then I think your impressions will change, but I don't propose to bias your mind by suggesting how that change may come, or what form it will take. Explore the valley for yourself tomorrow and then, if you should feel so disposed, I should be most interested to hear your views. As to your second question,' he went on, 'I regret the remark, and do not know what prompted me to make it. I would prefer not to explain myself further for the moment, except to suggest that a belief in heaven implies a corresponding belief in hell.'

Despite renewed questioning, the older man refused to commit himself further, and it was a puzzled and thoughtful Carfax who eventually bid his fellow-guest good night, lit his candle, and made his way up the narrow, stone newel stair to his bed in the tower room.

He slept soundly, rose early and breakfasted alone. He was about to set out on his tour of exploration, in fact he was standing in the hall of the inn packing sandwiches into his haversack, when he noticed the visitors' book and remembered that he had not yet signed it. As he turned the pages to remedy this omission, he discovered the identity of his fellow-guest, for in the last occupied space was written 'Charles Elphinstone, Oxford', in a fluent, scholarly hand. The name seemed familiar, but for the life of him he could not place it.

By the time he had reached the valley floor the previous night, darkness had prevented him from forming an adequate picture of his new surroundings, and now the weather conditions could scarcely have been less favourable. The portents of a stormy sunset and an ominously clear night had been fulfilled. The mountain walls upon either hand were hidden by a moving wrack of clouds whose tattered fringe had descended almost to the upper limit of the cultivated fields. A fine but deceptively penetrating rain was falling, and although occasional strong gusts of wind came eddying off the mountains, now from this direction, now from that, the air was humid and stifling. The swollen Garon and the innumerable small torrents cascading down the steep slopes filled the valley with the sound of falling water. Nevertheless, knowing how swiftly the mountain climate could change, Carfax was not unduly downcast and, buttoning up the collar of his mackintosh, he set off resolutely up the valley. The lane was narrow and high banked, and was never far away from the line of alder and hazel which overhung the shallow gorge through which the river flowed. He noticed that the small fields, both pasture and arable, looked clean and well tended, their hedges neatly laid and trimmed, but he saw no one at work in them. The small farms seemed equally deserted, and had he not scented wood-smoke as he passed them he would have thought that they were empty. No doubt the weather accounted for this suspension of activity. It struck him as ironical that the only fellow-mortal he encountered in the morning's solitude he passed by unawares. Only a chance glance over his shoulder had revealed the figure of a man sheltering beneath a tree which he had lately passed. The man stood so still, and the old brown overcoat, together with the sack which he had thrown over head and shoulders against the wet, blended so exactly with the colour of the tree bole at his back, that Carfax stopped for a moment to confirm his first glance. The man ignored his scrutiny, but when, at the bend of the road, he looked back again, he was no longer to be seen.

He had been walking for the best part of an hour when he saw on the left of the road what he took to be the ruins of a church. The valley was narrower here, and its walls more precipitous, for the clouds revealed glimpses of naked crags and desolate screes of shattered boulders. As though these features had not already made the site of the church sombre enough, a dense belt of pine-trees had been planted beside it. This must be Capel Cwm Garon, he reflected, recalling his study of the map during breakfast. He thought he had never seen so gloomy a place, it would seem dark even in sunlight, and, as the ruined church appeared to be of no architectural merit, he walked on. He conjectured that he must be nearing the head of the valley, for the lane grew rougher and commenced to climb steeply until he presently gained the open mountain. The rain had stopped, the sky looked brighter ahead, while the clouds showed no signs of lifting. The rain, the lowering clouds and the oppressive humid warmth of the valley had between them damped his spirits, but now he stepped out cheerfully, a cooler and drier wind in his face which made him feel as one who passes into fresh night air out of some overheated room.

By the time he had reached the head of the pass and could look down on the great landscape of hill and vale spread out beneath him, there was blue sky overhead, and a moving pattern of sunlight and shadow was dappling the slopes of the mountains. Carfax felt very well content as he sat with his back against a sheltering boulder and munched his sandwiches. Not far away a little group of mountain ponies were grazing, while high overhead a buzzard soared on moth-like wings. A shepherd was gathering his sheep off the north face of the mountain; Carfax could see his tiny foreshortened figure on the plateau far below, and his shrill whistle as he worked his dogs was borne up to him on the wind. These things brought a sense of life and companionship, dispelling the feeling of loneliness that had been growing upon him since he left the train on the previous day. He took out his map and checked his position. He had reached the central massif of the range. From it, the long ridges stretched southward like the fingers of an outspread hand. Between them, and to the west, lay two valleys, the Llan Fawr and the Llan Fechan, running parallel with Cwm Garon. As the weather seemed to have set fair, and there was plenty of time, he decided he would walk back down the Llan Fawr valley, cross the intervening ridge at a point well below Llangaron, and so return to the inn from the opposite direction.

He found that the valley of Llan Fawr was physically very similar to that of Cwm Garon. If anything, it was even narrower, while the mountain walls were equally high. Yet somehow the atmosphere of the place seemed quite different; 'more friendly' was the description which at once occurred to him. Obviously the improvement in the weather must be responsible, he decided; this mountain country was strangely temperamental. Owing to the more restricted area of cultivated land, the small farms were spaced farther apart than those in Cwm Garon, yet there seemed to be no lack of life and activity. A hedger at work beside the lane, and a swarthy individual leading a pair of jennets with pack-saddles, bid him a lilting good day as he passed. In one farmyard three small children paused from play to stare round-eyed as he went by, while in a nearby field, sown with oats, a farmer was working a two-horse roll. Finally, just before he turned off the road to climb back over the ridge, he met a woman driving three cows to the evening milking.

When he had finished the climb and begun the steep descent, the sun was still lighting the fields on the farther side of Cwm Garon, but he noticed that they looked just as deserted as they had done that morning. There still seemed to be neither sight nor sound of any activity. Silence seemed to well up from the valley like water from a spring, in fact the distant murmur of the Garon seemed to symbolize and accentuate it. He began to recall all the small workaday noises which he had heard but not remarked in Llan Fawr, and the lower he descended, the louder his foot-falls seemed to sound. Despite the sunlight and the clear air he found the feeling of loneliness and of strange oppression inexplicably returning. There was a sense of menacing constriction about the towering walls which hemmed in this valley and cut him off from the outer world, and yet, after his experience in Llan Fawr, he knew that it could not merely be a case of claustrophobia.

He had not gone far along the road back to Llangaron when he came in sight of a small public-house, and decided that a glass of beer would help him over the last lap of the way. Probably, too, he would find company there which would dispel this curious illusion that the valley was deserted.

The dim, low-ceilinged room – there was no bar – was snug and spotless. The stone-flagged floor looked newly scrubbed, and the dark polished surfaces of table, settle and high-backed Welsh dresser caught the light of the cheerful fire which burned in the hob grate. But the room was empty and silent save for the small settling sounds of the fire and the measured ticking of the grandfather clock. Carfax coughed and scuffed his feet on the flags. A latch clicked in the back of the house, and as the unseen door opened he heard a deep rumble of male voices. A woman appeared, and when she had fetched his drink he made some trivial pleasantry, but she seemed either shy or taciturn, for she answered in monosyllables, and after standing awkwardly for a moment, retired again to what he imagined to be the kitchen. The indistinguishable murmur of male talk went on. Carfax took a deep and gratifying draught, and then stooped to knock out his pipe in the ashtray. As he did so, he realized that the dottle already in the tray was warm, and that the cigarette stub beside it was still smouldering. Looking round the room curiously, he then saw that a man's cap lay in the chimney-corner of the settle, and that two knarled hazel sticks were propped against the wall near the door. At any other time and place, Carfax would not have observed such trivialities, and even if he had he would have attached no importance to them. But now they bred in him a disquieting suspicion which refused to be dispelled. It was that his approach had been discreetly observed by the late occupants of the room, and that for reasons best known to themselves they had retreated to the kitchen. The uncomfortable feeling of unwelcome intrusion which this suspicion prompted scarcely encouraged him to linger. The room seemed to have grown suddenly hostile, so much so that he did not even pause to refill his pipe, but drained his glass and set out once more upon his way.

The sunlight had now crept away from the fields, so that although the higher slopes of the eastern ridge were still suffused with golden light, the shadows in the valley were already thickening into twilight. His experience at the inn had exerted a curious influence over his mind, he discovered, for although the farms he passed seemed as still and deserted as those he had seen that morning, they no longer gave him the impression of being uninhabited. On the contrary, he imagined that every window concealed a watcher, that every house was the centre of some intense and secret life which, at his approach, was instantly suspended. The farther he went the more certain did he become that his every movement was the subject of furtive scrutiny, yet it was a certainty which his reason was powerless either to confirm or to disprove. Time and again he would stop and look back quickly, hoping to surprise the swaying of a curtain, the movement of a door, or to see in the shadows of tree or hedge some tangible shape. He looked in vain. Yet the feeling and the fear continued to grow upon him despite his senses' negative evidence. It was no longer confined to the houses he passed and to the people who might or might not lurk within them; it was a fear distilled by the valley itself. The brooding mountains, the still pines, even the heavy, windless air itself seemed to have suspended some secret activity to join in this silent and malign watch. As he walked resolutely on, fear stalked at his elbow, and he felt as if he was the focal point of some great burning-glass of hostile forces. Just as the first lightning flash and thunder-clap puts a welcome end to the breath-bating suspense that precedes the storm, Carfax found himself wishing that something, however fearful, might happen. But no material event took place, and he reached the inn at Llangaron in good time for dinner. In the cheerful light of the dining-room he felt inclined to dismiss the matter as so much hallucination, but he could not deny that, as his fellow-guest had prophesied, his first impression of the valley had undergone radical revision.

'Well,' queried Elphinstone as they drew their chairs to the fire after dinner, 'what's the verdict now?'

Carfax hesitated. Considered in retrospect, his fears seemed so intangible and groundless, that he felt foolish and doubted his ability to express them in so many words. With the other's encouragement, however, he presently gave as detailed and faithful an account of his day as he was able. During his narration Elphinstone nodded occasionally, but seemed to evince no surprise. When Carfax had finished speaking he remained silent for a few moments, pulling at a thin, black cheroot.

'Interesting,' he said at length. 'Very interesting, but not, I can assure you, a unique experience by any means. For years, I might safely say for centuries, strangers have been made aware, by some such means as you describe, that they were not welcome in this valley.'

'But it's not just the people,' put in Carfax. 'It's as though the valley . . .'

'I know, I know,' the older man cut him short. 'It's not as simple as that, is it? "An angel satyr walks these hills",' he quoted; 'know who wrote that? Why Kilvert. "Angel satyr" – a curious association of opposites – what do you suppose induced a mild little Victorian curate to use such a term?'

'I think I can understand now,' Carfax admitted. 'And yet,' he went on, 'I refuse to believe that this sense of evil is a natural emanation of the place itself. As a Christian, I hold that both good and evil are human concepts, and that they do not exist in nature.'

'Well put,' said the other, 'and probably true, but if, as a Christian, you believe that there are spiritual as well as material powers, then don't you think it possible that man might abuse and pervert the former no less than the latter?'

Carfax nodded. 'Yes,' he agreed, thoughtfully, 'I suppose such a thing is possible.'

'I am sure of it,' Elphinstone went on, 'and what's more I consider that this valley can prove my contention.'

'Go on,' prompted Carfax.

'I believe,' the other continued, 'that some evil force dominates Cwm Garon. I think it is a natural force which man, in some remote time, released and harnessed to secret and perverted ends. For centuries this dark power has been, as it were, dammed up in this valley until it has soaked into the very stones of the place. That is why a more superficial mind than yours might imagine that it is a natural phenomenon. Outside interference has an effect upon it like that of a stone flung into a still pool. That's why Cwm Garon and its people have always implacably resisted intrusion.' He paused.

'But is that really so?' queried Carfax. 'What evidence have you?'

'Apart from many similar experiences to your own,' the older man replied, 'there is ample historical evidence. Take this Abbey, for instance.' He made a sweeping gesture. 'It did not survive until the Dissolution. What happened? The community dwindled. Its numbers could not be maintained. Finally, a new Abbey of Llangaron was built in the safe, flat lands beside the Wye, and the old was abandoned. It has been said that it was too solitary, too open to attack by wolves or raiding hillmen. Do you find that explanation convincing? Do you think that a Church which deliberately sought the solitudes, and which established flourishing communities at such places as Valle Crucis or Strata Florida would be defeated merely by the loneliness of Cwm Garon? No, I suggest that they went because they feared something more potent but less tangible than wolves or robbers.

'You say you saw the ruined church at Capel Cwm Garon; do you know the history of that? It was built by a nineteenth-century religious sect headed by a man who called himself Brother Jeremy. What happened? History repeated itself; the community dwindled; misfortune followed misfortune. The eventual result you have seen for yourself. It's not only the efforts of the Church that have failed,' he went on. 'On the slope of the mountain just behind here you'll find the ruins of a house. There's not much to see, but it is all that's left of the place that Alaric Stephenson the artist tried to build for himself. I say "tried" because it was never finished. He apparently had some grandiose notion that he was going to make a sort of miniature paradise for himself here, but he soon found he was mistaken. Everything went wrong. No local contractors would work for him. What was done during the day was undone at night. Even the trees he tried to plant were uprooted. I could quote several other examples of the same kind of thing, but the repetition would be boring.'

'But do these . . . these forces manifest themselves in any way?' questioned Carfax.

'That depends,' was the answer. 'Unless you deliberately seek them or try to interfere with them, I should say no; you might stay here a month without experiencing any more than the sense of hostility and surveillance which you felt today!'

Elphinstone rose to his feet and lit the candle on the side-table.

'What is this extraordinary influence, and how exactly does it affect the people who live in Cwm Garon?' Carfax persisted.

The other was standing in the doorway about to bid him good night. His keen eyes glittered in the flickering candle flame as he smiled and shook his head.

'I cannot answer that question,' he replied. 'At least, not yet. I think I have a shrewd idea, but one day – soon perhaps – I hope to know.'

The conversation had filled Carfax's head with disturbing speculations, and despite his long day in the mountain air it was some time before he lost consciousness. Even so, it must have been a light doze instead of his usual sound sleep, for he presently awoke and, glancing at the luminous dial of his wrist-watch, saw that it was nearly midnight. He became aware of stealthy movement in the room overhead at the top of the tower, movement betrayed by sounds so slight he could never have detected them but for the profound silence. Then he heard the pad of stealthy feet descending the stone stairs. A thin pencil of light flickered momentarily beneath his door and was gone. Carfax climbed softly out of the bed and crossed to the open window. He was in time to see a tall, slightly stooping, figure which he recognized unmistakably as that of Charles Elphinstone, cross the grass below and disappear beyond the ruined wall of the cloister garth. As he watched, he suddenly recalled the association of the name which had eluded him all day – Professor Charles Elphinstone, probably the greatest authority on folklore and magic since Frazer. 'One day – soon perhaps – I hope to know.' He seemed to hear an echo of his last words. Though Carfax was by no means of a timid disposition, he felt a reluctant, even envious feeling of admiration for the intrepid old man. Admittedly, on the face of it, a midnight stroll in this quiet Welsh valley seemed to call for no particular display of courage. The night was clear and brightly moonlit, the scene the same as before, the same black shadows of the nave arches on the dew-laden grass, the same black grandeur of mountains framed in the gaping east window, the same stillness. Yet this time, Carfax had no thought of Vaughan or Traherne, for he knew the fear that lurked in this silence. Were those lights, moving and dancing along the slopes of the mountains, or was it merely a trick of moonlight shining upon stone? Somewhere near at hand an owl hooted mournfully, and there came into his mind a line from the thirteenth chapter of Isaiah: 'Owls shall dwell there, and satyrs shall dance there.' He shivered, and returned to the welcome warmth of the bed.

The Professor did not appear at breakfast. Doubtless he was making up for lost sleep thought Carfax, but the reflection could not dispel a vague sense of uneasiness which refused to be quieted. He deliberately loitered in the dining-room, hoping Elphinstone would come. When, at half-past ten, his place was still empty, Carfax determined to settle his fears. He climbed the tower stairs to the Professor's room. A can stood outside his door. It was full, and the water was quite cold. He knocked softly, then more loudly. There was no response. Turning the handle very gently he opened the door a few inches and looked in. The room was empty.

Some instinct prompted Carfax to set out on his search in the same direction as he had taken the previous day, towards the ruined church of Capel Cwm Garon. He was still trying to reassure himself that his fears were groundless. Though Elphinstone had not, it appeared, warned the inn of any intended absence, he might well have decided to stay out on such a fine morning, while even involuntary absence might be caused by no worse mishap than a sprained ankle. Yet the feeling of foreboding would not be appeased. He realized that the date was May the first, that last night, in fact, had been 'Eve of May' of ancient celebration, and somehow this knowledge by no means allayed his concern. Meanwhile, his senses observed the same atmosphere of hostility and watchfulness, but now, pre-occupied with fresh fears, he no longer turned to peer at vacant windows or into the shadows beneath the trees, knowing that to do so would be fruitless. So he strode on until he came in sight of the crags of Black Daren which towered above the ruined church. As his eyes roamed over the precipice, he thought he detected a movement among the boulders of the screes below. He fumbled for his binoculars, and focused them hurriedly. Two men appeared to be bending over something which lay behind a rock, invisible to him. 'No doubt a sheep has fallen from the crags,' whispered reason, but dread lent wings to his feet.

Professor Charles Elphinstone had obviously slipped and fallen from a great height in attempting to scale the crags, and his body lay against the rock in that attitude of macabre abandonment which betokens shattered bones. His hat had fallen off, and the luxuriant white hair was matted with congealed blood. Carfax, who was familiar with death in many forms, was not dismayed by these gruesome commonplaces of violent dissolution. What drained the blood from his face and impelled him quickly to replace the sack which covered the body, was the expression on the face. He would not have believed that the features he had lately seen so calm and self confident, could have been moulded by terror to such hideous contortion.

It may be thought that Carfax would have no desire ever to revisit the valley; he would certainly have subscribed to this view himself when he left Llangaron on the day following the tragic accident. Everything about Cwm Garon had become repulsive to him and, as many others, it seemed, had done before him, he retired defeated. Never did the mundane environment of the outside world seem so friendly and welcoming. When the train pulled in to the little station at Pont Newydd he could scarcely resist the impulse to run up to the footplate and shake the driver by the hand. Yet – and to those who have never visited Cwm Garon this will seem the most improbable part of this strange story – as the weeks went by after his return to London, fear turned to curiosity, and repulsion to an attraction which he found increasingly difficult to resist. It was almost as though some powerful influence was luring him back.

Be that as it may, Carfax did return to the valley, and a sultry night on the eve of August the first found him once again walking up the lane toward Capel Cwm Garon. The heat in the valley that day had been stifling. Everything had felt hot to the touch, and the outlines of the mountain ridges shimmered in a haze which mingled with the acrid smoke of a heather fire. Never had the atmosphere seemed so surcharged with still suspense. Even the interminable voice of the Garon had been muted by weeks of drought. Only occasionally, far away over the mountains toward Radnor, faint thunder growled and muttered. At evening a grey veil of cloud had spread slowly across the sky so that the night fell black and starless. Yet the heat was still insufferable and there was no breath of wind. Everything, from towering mountain to individual leaf or grass blade, seemed poised in tense expectancy as though awaiting some tremendous event.

I will not attempt to analyse Carfax's state of mind as he strode on through the dark of the high-banked lane. Though still beyond the reach of his five senses, his reason no longer questioned the reality of a malign, unsleeping watch. Yet still, 'For lust of knowing what should not be known', he held on purposefully. Somewhere above the invisible crags of the Black Daren a heather fire was still burning, a livid wheal of flickering flame twisting snake-like across the face of the mountains. But Carfax also saw other lights in the darkness, moving points of light which no comfortable theory could explain. They appeared to move swiftly along and down the mountain walls, converging, it would seem, upon the church at Capel Cwm Garon. There must, he thought, be another fire just beyond the church, for the ruined walls were visible against its dull red glare. As he approached more closely, however, he saw, with a new fear stirring in his heart, that he was mistaken, and that the light was actually coming from within the church itself.

While fascination fought with terror within him he drew nearer, leaving the lane for the short turf of the field where his footfalls made no sound, until he reached a position from which he could see into the roofless nave. In the centre of the church stood a brazier which glowed redly and sent up swirling clouds of smoke whose pungent aromatic odour drifted across to where Carfax stood. Around and about the brazier moved a considerable company of men and women. They were naked, and as they moved, their bodies seemed to capture and reflect the ruddy glare of the fire as though they were lacquered. When he glimpsed them momentarily in the firelight, Carfax thought that the faces of a few of the taller ones seemed vaguely familiar, but the majority of the company appeared to be very short in stature, so short, in fact, that at the first instant of vision he thought they must be children. Their bodies, however, belied this impression, as did their faces, for their countenances were such that Carfax was grateful for the smoke which prevented him from seeing them clearly. Sometimes the company moved in slow and stately dance, sometimes the pace quickened to a frenzy accompanied by gesture and posture indescribably obscene. Naked feet moved silently and there was no sound of music, yet always they seemed obedient to the measure of some inaudible rhythm. Now and again the smoke whirled aside to reveal, in the shadows beyond the brazier, a horned figure seated upon some kind of throne. Carfax marked this inhuman shape with a renewed access of fear until he realized that it was a man clothed in skins and wearing a horned head-dress. He knew then that he was beholding the celebration of rites unbelievably ancient, and temporarily his interest overcame his revulsion and his fear. But only momentarily, for it dawned upon him that this spectacle, for all its diabolic depravity, was human, and that it inspired a purely physical emotion, whereas the malignant power which brooded over the valley itself was something more or less than human. These forms which writhed in the firelight might conjure or appease that power, but they were not the power itself; their monstrous celebration had not abated the tense expectancy of the stillness. The valley still awaited some greater event.

Suddenly, a blinding flash of lightning, followed immediately by a crash of thunder tore through the veil of darkness and silence. Reverberating like great drums, the mountains took up the roar of sound and flung it from wall to wall, echoing and re-echoing down Cwm Garon. The figures round the fire had ceased their dance and flung themselves prostrate on the ground. The fire itself burnt low. The thunder died away with a sound like the closing of some vast door, and with its passing there seized Carfax a terror of the soul so abject that it was as though the valley yawned like the mouth of hell. For there fell about him a silence that was like the soundless desolation of outer space, and a sightless darkness blacker than any midnight. Though his eyes were blinded and his ears heard no sound, he knew that there stalked through the valley something intangible, unearthly, monstrous and very terrible. Though no leaf moved, something stirred in his hair. It seemed to pass as a storm cloud passes, sweeping down Cwm Garon, and with that passage the spell which had bound senses and held limbs from motion lifted. Carfax screamed, and, slipping and stumbling, he ran towards the crags of Black Daren. At the sound of his voice, two squat figures left the circle round the fire. Their pale forms glimmered in the darkness as they followed lithely after, moving in swift silence over the screes.

A VISITOR AT ASHCOMBE

Ashcombe is a fine example of the smaller stone-built manor-house, a type in which the Cotswold country of Gloucestershire is peculiarly rich. I need not specify the precise location of the house beyond saying that it is not many miles from Stow-on-the-Wold. The local saying:

> 'Stow-on-the-Wold
> Where the wind blows cold'

is true enough in winter when the east winds whip across leagues of undulating, dry-walled uplands. Yet the stranger who travels in winter along one of the main roads which stride across these high wolds obtains a false impression of treeless bleakness. For they conceal within their folds many warm and sheltered combes in which the grey villages and farms lie snugly, linked to the great ridge roads by narrow, break-neck lanes. In such a sheltered and secluded site stands Ashcombe Manor, protected from the north and east, not only by the swell of the wolds, but by hanging beechwoods which flame with colour in autumn. The gabled front faces south down the combe, and the windows, with their stone mullions and hood moulds, look out over a smooth lawn and a strip of unfenced common to the village church. The view is uninterrupted because the lawn ends in a ha-ha, but the road discreetly skirts the edge of the common on its way to the little village which lies beyond the church.

For some years now the Manor has stood empty. Old Mrs Greening at the lodge keeps the key and, provided the old lady has not stepped down for a gossip or a dish of tea with her sister who keeps the village shop, the house is open to public inspection with the exception of one room on the ground floor. Empty country houses are no rarity in these highly taxed and servantless days, but, unlike the majority, Ashcombe is of small size and convenient plan, so that many visitors must have speculated on the reason for its desertion. Their curiosity goes unsatisfied. The more inquisitive may discover the belief, held by a few of the older villagers, that the house is haunted, a rumour which frequently attaches itself to an old, empty house and which, in this case, appears to have no specific foundation either in fact or folklore. If old Mrs Greening knows any more than the rest of the village she does not betray the fact.

'Ghosts!' she will exclaim contemptuously when taxed with the rumour, 'Ah, I a' seen plenty on 'em – four-footed 'uns wi' long tails, that's all as 'aunts Ashcombe. Old 'Lisha Peart's bin tellin' you the tale down the "Penderville", I can see. That owd rascal 'ud see Owd Nick hisself fer a pint o' scrumpy.'

Other obvious sources of information are not readily available. The present owner, young Dick Penderville, is in the Forces overseas, and in any case he has never lived in the house. The last tenants, Mr and Mrs Amos Bingley, an elderly childless couple, are now dead.

Amos Bingley was a typical example of the successful Black Country manufacturer. His career began at the early age of eight, when he worked as bellows-boy in his father's back-yard chain forge at Cradley Heath. It ended after the First World War, when he ceased to take an active part in the affairs of Messrs Amos Bingley and Company, Chain and Shackle Makers, and retired with a small, but adequate fortune. Sentiment, or more probably a folk memory derived from ancestors who combined chain-making with agriculture in days before the Black Country was black, had given him a craving for country life which he was at last able to satisfy by playing the country squire at Ashcombe. He cut a strange figure in this rôle, a squat figure of uncouth gait and with a bull-neck so short as to convey the impression of stooping, and to conceal from the casual glance the great breadth of shoulder and depth of chest. His enormous hands, obviously better fitted to grasp a sledge-hammer than a walking-stick, had never lost their callouses, nor his tongue its broad dialect. He made no attempt to ape the gentry, and while the vicar and the local 'county' regarded him askance, the villagers respected him, for forthrightness is a quality which the countryman has always cherished in himself and admired in others. His fierce Calvinistic piety brought a new lease of life to the little stone chapel opposite the 'Penderville Arms' and still further antagonized the vicar who believed that the Manor should be the pillar of the church. But while Amos Bingley may thus be said to have feared God, he certainly feared nothing else, or rather he did not do so until he came to Ashcombe. I do not know whether, at the time he took up his tenancy, he heard any rumour concerning the house, but if he had I do not doubt that his reaction would have been similar to that of old Mrs Greening, though couched in even more forceful language. In his rough passage through life he had encountered no power that a hard head or great physical strength could not match. His religion might smoulder with threats of hell-fire, but outside the four walls of the chapel he recognized no fires other than the white-hot reality of his furnace flames. It is a strange paradox that after a lifetime spent amid surroundings resembling Dante's Inferno, this tough old Black Countryman should have met his match in this quiet Cotswold village.

Mr Amos Bingley is now beyond question, but even if time or circumstance permitted, it is very doubtful if he would have been capable of giving any coherent account of his experience. For Mr Bingley's tenure was briefly, summarily and painfully terminated. Two years, almost to the day, after he first crossed the threshold of his new home, he left Ashcombe in a strait-jacket to die a few months later in Barnwell Asylum. This shocking event was the occasion of much comment in the district at the time. The villagers declared that he had suddenly lost all his money, and that the shock had proved too much for him. The parson regarded the event as evidence of the perils of non-conformity, while the gentry dismissed a distressing subject simply with a lift of the eyebrows and a significant movement of the elbow. But, in fact, the fortunes of Bingley and Company were as prosperous as ever, while although old Amos had been given to drinking-bouts in his younger days, he had grown abstemious with years for, like many men of his occupation, the chapel had taken the place of the public-house. The unfortunate Mrs Bingley left the district at once and went to live with her sister in Dudley, where she did not long survive her husband.

Apart from a few scraps of information grudgingly wrung from old Mrs Greening at the Lodge, our only clues to the peculiar events which seem to have occurred at Ashcombe Manor in the years 1922 and 1923 are contained in the weekly letters which Mrs Bingley wrote to her sister, and which the latter fortunately preserved.

It appears that for the first few months all went well; Mrs Bingley's letters describe in detail the process of domestic settlement and re-arrangement. It seems that Amos possessed an able partner who was not slow to stamp Ashcombe with the impress of her determined personality. Although the house was already partly furnished, the new tenants apparently imported a great deal of their own in addition, and I suspect that the result was enough to make the dim shapes of long dead Pendervilles start from those heavy-gilded frames which still hang above the oak staircase. The work of transforming Ashcombe to conform with Mrs Bingley's notions of domestic comfort was largely entrusted to Mrs Greening. It is clear that this formidable old retainer was too freely inclined to express ideas of her own which did not always agree with those of her new mistress. 'She will keep on with her: "Old Sir John used to say this", or "Old Sir John would never have had that", until I could clout her,' wrote Eliza Bingley. Nevertheless, no serious clash between the two women occurred until, nine months after her arrival, Mrs Bingley decided to use the Arms room.

The Arms room at Ashcombe is situated at the south-east angle of the building and on the ground floor. It has one large window facing east, and originally possessed a second, smaller window looking south across lawn and common to the church. This south window, however, has been blocked up owing, it is commonly supposed, to the window-tax. Whoever was responsible for this alteration was evidently anxious that it should not disfigure the balance of the façade, for the glazed casement has been retained in front of the infilling, an expedient which is quite successful. Seen from the common, the sham window easily escapes notice, and it is only on closer approach that it becomes apparent that the Manor possesses a 'blind eye'. A similar attempt at disguise has been made upon the inside. Here a second casement has been inserted and glazed with mirrors which, by their reflection, effectually lighten the deep embrasure in which the window is set. The effect is curious, the stranger approaching the window obliquely being startled to find himself confronted by his own image. In the centre of the panelled wall, directly opposite the mirror window stands the fireplace. It is surmounted by an unusually rich Jacobean overmantel. Upon this appear, in centre and flanking panels, the arms of the Pendervilles and of the families with whom they were linked by marriage.

Anyone who has been to Ashcombe will appreciate the necessity for this description because the Arms room is not open to inspection by the casual visitor on the grounds that certain intimate and valuable family possessions are stored there.

When the Bingleys came to Ashcombe, the Arms room was locked, but it was not long before the indefatigable Eliza, anxious to survey every cranny of her new domain, was rattling the latch of the door. Where was the key? Mrs Greening grudgingly admitted that it must be down at the Lodge. Later, however, she confessed that she must have mislaid it, and, in the general turmoil of moving in, the subject of the locked room was shelved. But only temporarily, Mrs Bingley was not to be put off so easily, and soon, in response to her renewed demands, Mrs Greening was compelled to find the key. Although the room was quite unfurnished and had obviously been unoccupied for many years, the great fireplace appealed to Mrs Bingley's ideas of manorial grandeur, and she resolved forthwith that this should be her dining-room. Her decision was not without good reason. The existing dining-room faced south and west whereas, she argued, the Arms room would catch all the morning sun, and yet remain pleasantly cool and shaded on hot summer evenings. Mrs Greening, however, thought otherwise, and did not hesitate to say so in no uncertain terms. Her reasons, that Sir John had never used the room, and that it was 'a nasty, dark, cold, smelly old place, anyway', were not sufficient to deter Mrs Bingley, and old Mrs Greening was forced to retire discomfited from an encounter which would have cost most servants their place.

In fact, like her husband, Eliza Bingley seems to have possessed a will which thrived on opposition. After an orgy of scrubbing and polishing, the Arms room took on a new lease of life, and soon the Black Country chain-maker was sitting down to dine in his baronial hall beneath the carved bearings of his forerunners. The room may have been a little gloomy, as Mrs Greening had said, but it certainly was not cold. In fact, as Mrs Bingley told her sister, with a great log-fire blazing in the open hearth, it was apt to grow almost uncomfortably warm. But these were matters of little or no account; a feature of the room which caused more concern was an unpleasant smell which was occasionally noticeable. When Mrs Greening had referred to the room as 'a smelly old place' she may not have used the epithet in a strictly literal sense, and it was certainly not understood in such a light. Nevertheless, the fact remains that the room did smell. At first, Mrs Bingley identified it as the stale odour of previous meals hanging in the air owing to inadequate ventilation, and she ordered the window to be opened wide whenever the room was unoccupied. Apparently this expedient proved ineffective, for we soon find Mrs Bingley tracing the source of the trouble to the fireplace. Some sort of interference between the dining-room and kitchen flues was suspected. Builder and sweep were called in, patent cowls were fitted to both chimneys, and the cook was ordered to stop using the kitchen range as an incinerator for scraps of meat or old bones, a practice she apparently denied with some heat, although charged with it on more than one occasion. Yet despite these efforts the source of the trouble was still elusive. The nuisance was not constant. Sometimes it was unnoticeable, while at others, usually towards evening, the unplesant odour became so strong that a less determined woman than Eliza Bingley might have abandoned the room. To have done so, however, would have meant admitting defeat to Mrs Greening, and that she would never do. Even the first curious incidents connected with the mirror window did not shake her stubbornness. Attributing her experience to defective vision, she announces her intention of visiting an oculist in Cheltenham, and, in her next letter, assigns a similar hallucination of her husband's to the same cause. Whether this explanation really satisfied her we cannot know.

She had had occasion to return to the Arms room after dinner. It was the month of February, and the room was lit only by the firelight. (There was no electric light at Ashcombe in those days.) She noticed that the smell was unpleasantly strong and resolved to tax the cook once more with burning rubbish in the range. As she passed by, she happened to glance into the embrasure of the mirror window, and saw the flickering firelight reflected in the glass. It was only a momentary glance, and it was not until she was out of the room that it occurred to her that there was anything odd about what she had seen. Then she realized that as she had crossed directly between the fireplace and the window, she should have seen her silhouette reflected in the mirror, whereas she could swear that all she had noticed was the uninterrupted reflection of the fire. Her husband's experience a few days later was complicated by another strange feature. Not only did the mirror window fail to record old Amos, but he swore positively, and with some force, that whereas the real fire had been reduced to a few red embers, the reflected fire burned brightly so that the room was illuminated, not so much by the fireplace, as by a ruddy glare which streamed from the mirror.

An unpleasant smell and an optical illusion; these were apparently the only incidents which gave warning of the sequel which Mrs Bingley records, ungrammatically and often scarcely legibly, in her last letter. It was only when she was preparing for bed, she writes, that she remembered that she had left her bag on her chair in the Arms room. The smell was stronger than she had ever known it, but the fire had burned low and she noticed with relief that no bright glare, such as her husband had described, shone out of the embrasure. It, too, was dark. Emboldened, she determined to dispose of her previous illusion, and, standing directly before the fireplace, she looked into the mirror for her reflection. It was not there. She turned away hurriedly and groped for her bag, but when she re-passed the window she could not resist a second glance. This time a dark shape partly obscured the reflected firelight. Her first feeling was one of relief until, like a child making shadow-pictures, she waved her hand and wagged her head idiotically from side to side. The form in the mirror did not move, and there dawned upon her with dreadful certainty the conviction that the mirror was no longer a mirror but a window; that the fire which glowed there was not the fire which burned in the room; that the shadow she saw there was not her shadow. The tables were now turned upon her for, while terror held her motionless, the shadow began to move. Though the light was too dim to disinguish detail of form or movement, yet both contrived to convey an intensity of purpose which was horribly confirmed by faint scratching and pattering sounds, as if nails scratched upon the glass of a window and clawed the putty from the panes. At this, Mrs Bingley recovered the use of her limbs, and in less time than it takes to tell she was back in the drawing-room, trembling from head to foot and obviously on the verge of collapse.

Ignoring her hysterical efforts to dissuade him, old Amos Bingley got up from his chair, seized the heavy poker from the hearth in one great hand and the lamp in the other, and set off down the passage. What went on inside the Arms room then we can only conjecture. Eliza says she heard the heavy door flung open and then slammed shut with a force which shook the house. This was followed by a prolonged series of sickening thuds and crashes accompanied by the voice of Amos bellowing inarticulately like an enraged bull. Yet what apparently frightened Mrs

Bingley much more was a fainter, sibilant kind of noise which all this hubbub and commotion could not quite drown. Although she could distinguish no words it sounded, to use her own description, 'as if someone who had lost their voice was trying to shout'. At length, she heard Amos Bingley cry out more loudly than ever in a tone she had never heard before, and then complete silence fell upon the house.

By this time the cook and the housemaid had joined Mrs Bingley in the drawing-room, but it was some time before the white-faced trio could pluck up the courage to creep down the corridor to the Arms room. They were confronted with a scene of indescribable confusion. The furniture was smashed to matchwood. Even the panelling exhibits to this day the marks of the blows of the poker which lay in a corner of the room, twisted as though it had been a length of lead piping. In the midst of a welter of splintered wood, crumpled carpet, torn curtains and broken china, Amos Bingley lay insensible, his face a rigid mask of terrified fury. He had evidently been burned by the smashed lamp, for his clothes were smouldering, while his hands were blistered and blackened as though he had plunged them into a fire. The sickly stench in the room was intolerable.

I have no positive explanation to offer for this strange story, although the following fruits of local archaeological research may possibly have some bearing upon the matter.

The name 'Arms room' would appear to be of comparatively recent origin for, in an eighteenth-century inventory of the Manor which the agent courteously permitted me to examine, it is referred to as 'Sir Neville's Parlour'. This presumably commemorates Sir Neville Penderville (1576–1639) who became Lord of the Manor of Ashcombe in 1608, and who was commended by James I for his zeal as a magistrate.

From a study of the Manorial Rolls it transpires that Matthew Hopkins, the celebrated (or infamous) witchfinder, visited the neighbourhood in 1637, and that as a result Deborah Golightly, described as an elderly widow living alone at Hobs Cottage, Ashcombe Bottom, was arraigned, tried and convicted of the practice of witchcraft and necromancy. She was sentenced to death by hanging, her body to be subsequently burned, these enactments being shortly afterwards carried out 'upon the common called the Church Common in the parish of Ashcombe.'

THE GARSIDE FELL DISASTER

'Yes, I'm an old railwayman I am, and proud of it. You see, I come of a railway family, as you might say, for I reckon there've been Boothroyds on the railway – in the signal cabin or on the footplate mostly – ever since old Geordie Stevenson was about. We haven't always served the same company. There were four of us. My two elder brothers followed my father on the North-Western, but I joined the Grand Trunk, and Bert, our youngest, he went east to Grantham. He hadn't been long there before he was firing on one of Patrick Stirling's eight-foot singles, the prettiest little locos as ever was or ever will be I reckon. He finished up driver on Ivatt's "Atlantics" while Harry and Fred were working "Jumbos" and "Precursors" out of Crewe. I could have had the footplate job myself easy enough if I'd a mind; took it in with my mother's milk I did, if you follow my meaning. But (and sometimes I'm not sure as I don't regret it) I married early on, and the old woman persuaded me to go for a more settled job, so it was the signal box for me. A driver's wife's a widow most o' the week, see, unless he happens to click for a regular local turn.

'The first job I had on my own was at Garside on the Carlisle line south of Highbeck Junction, and it was here that this business as I was speaking of happened; a proper bad do it was, and the rummest thing as ever I had happen in all my time.

'Now you could travel the railways from one end to t'other, Scotland and all, but I doubt you'd find a more lonesome spot than Garside, or one so mortal cold in winter. I don't know if you've ever travelled that road, but all I know is it must have cost a mint of money. You see, the Grand Trunk wanted their own road to Scotland, but the East Coast lot had taken the easiest pick, and the North-Western had the next best run through Preston and over Shap, so there was nothing else for them but to carry their road over the mountains. It took a bit of doing, I can tell you, and I know, for when I was up there, there was plenty of folks about who remembered the railway coming. They told me what a game it was what with the snow and the wind, and the clay that was like rock in summer and a treacle pudding in winter.

'Garside Box takes its name from Garside Fell same as the tunnel. There's no station there, for there isn't a house in sight, let alone a village, and my cottage was down at Frithdale about half an hour's walk away. It was what we call a section box, just a small box, the signals, and two "lie-by" roads, one on the up and one on the down side, where goods trains could stand to let the fast trains through if need be. Maybe you know how the block system works; how you can only admit one train on to a section at a time. Well, it would have been an eight-mile section, heavily graded at that, from Highbeck to Ennerthwaite, the next station south, and it might have taken a heavy goods anything up to half an hour to clear it. That's why they made two sections of it by building Garside box just midway between the two. It was over a thousand feet up, not far short of the summit of the line; in fact, looking south from my box I could see that summit, top of the long bank up from Ennerthwaite. Just north of the box was the mouth of the tunnel, a mile and a half of it, under Garside Fell. If ever you should come to walk over those mountains you couldn't miss the ventilation shafts of the tunnel. It looks kind of queer to see those great stone towers a-smoking and steaming away up there in the heather miles and miles from anywhere with not a soul for company and all so quiet. Not that they smoke now as much as they did, but I'll be coming to that presently.

'Well, as I've said before, you could travel the length and breadth of England before you'd find a lonelier place than Garside. Job Micklewright, who was ganger on the section, would generally give me a look up when he went by, and if I switched a goods into the "lie-by", more often than not the fireman or the guard would pass the time of day, give me any news from down the line, and maybe make a can of tea on my stove. But otherwise I wouldn't see a soul from the time I came on till I got my relief. Of course there was the trains, but then you couldn't call them company, not properly speaking. Hundreds and hundreds of folks must have passed me by every day, and yet there I was on my own with only a few old sheep for company, and the birds crying up on the moor. Funny that, when you come to think of it, isn't it? Mind you, I'm not saying it wasn't grand to be up there on a fine day in summer. You could keep your town life then. It made you feel as it was good to be alive what with the sun a-shining and the heather all out, grasshoppers ticking away and the air fairly humming with bees. Yes, you got to notice little things like that, and as for the smell of that moor in summer, why, I reckon I can smell it now. It was a different tale in winter though. Cold? It fair makes me shiver to think on it. I've known the wind set in the north-east for months on end, what we call a lazy wind – blows through you, see, too tired to go round. Sometimes it blew that strong it was all you could do to stand against it. More than once I had the glass of my windows blown in, and there were times when I thought the whole cabin was going what with the roaring and rattling and shaking of it. Just you imagine climbing a signal ladder to fix a lamp in that sort of weather; it wasn't easy to keep those lamps in, I can tell you. Then there was the snow; you don't know what snow is down here in the south. The company was well off for ploughs and we'd no lack of good engines even in those days, but it used to beat them. Why, I've known it snow for two days and a night, blowing half a gale all the while, and at the end of it there's been a drift of snow twenty feet deep in the cutting up by the tunnel.

'But in spite of all the wind and the snow and the rain (Lord, how it could rain!) it was the mists as I hated most. That may sound funny to you, but then no signalman can a-bear mist and fog, it kind of blinds you, and that makes you uneasy. It's for the signalman to judge whether he shall call out the fogmen, and that's a big responsibility. It may come up sudden after sundown in autumn, you calls your fogmen, and by the time they come on it's all cleared off and they want to know what the hell you're playing at. So another time you put off calling them, but it don't clear, and before you know where you are you've got trains over-running signals. We had no fogmen at Garside, there was little occasion for them, but we kept a box of detonators in the cabin. All the same, I didn't like fog no more for that. They're queer things are those mountain mists. Sometimes all day I'd see one hanging on the moor, perhaps only a hundred yards away, but never seeming to come no nearer. And then all on a sudden down it would come so thick that in a minute, no more, I couldn't see my home signals. But there was another sort of fog at Garside that I liked even less, and that was the sort that came out from the tunnel. Ah! now that strikes you as funny, doesn't it? Maybe you're thinking that with such a lonesome job I took to fancying things. Oh, I know, I know, if you're a nervy chap it's easy to see things in the mist as have no right to be there, or to hear queer noises when really it's only the wind shouting around or humming in the wires. But I wasn't that sort, and what's more I wasn't the only one who found out that there was something as wasn't quite right about Garside. No, you can take it from me that what I'm telling you is gospel, as true as I'm sitting in this bar a-talking to you.

'No doubt you've often looked at the mouth of a railway tunnel and noticed how the smoke comes a-curling out even though there may not be a sight or sound of any traffic. Well, the first thing I noticed about Garside tunnel was that, for all its ventilation shafts, it was the smokiest hole I'd ever seen. Not that this struck me as queer, at least not at first. I remember, though, soon after I came there I was walking up from Frithdale one Monday morning for the early turn and saw that number two shaft way up on the fell was smoking like a factory chimney. That did seem a bit strange, for there was precious little traffic through on a

Sunday in those days; in fact, Garside box was locked out and they worked the full eight-mile section. Still, I didn't give much thought to it until one night about three weeks later. It was almost dark, but not so dark that I couldn't just see the tunnel mouth and the whitish-looking smoke sort of oozing out of it. Now, both sections were clear, mind; the last train through had been an up Class A goods and I'd had the "out of section" from Highbeck south box a good half-hour before. But, believe it or not, that smoke grew more and more as I watched it. At first I thought it must be a trick of the wind blowing through the tunnel, though the air seemed still enough for once in a way. But it went on coming out thicker and thicker until I couldn't see the tunnel itself at all, and it came up the cutting toward my box for all the world like a wall of fog. One minute there was a clear sky overhead, the next minute – gone – and the smell of it was fit to choke you. Railway tunnels are smelly holes at the best of times, but that smell was different somehow, and worse than anything I've ever struck. It was so thick round my box that I was thinking of looking out my fog signals, when a bit of a breeze must have got up, for all on a sudden it was gone as quick as it came. The moon was up, and there was the old tunnel plain in the moonlight, just smoking away innocent like as though nothing had happened. Fair made me rub my eyes. "Alf," I say to myself, "you've been dreaming," but all the while I knew I hadn't.

'At first I thought I'd best keep it to myself, but the same thing happened two or three times in the next month or so until one day, casual like, I mentioned it to Perce Shaw who was my relief. He'd had it happen, too, it seemed, but like me he hadn't felt like mentioning it to anyone. "Well," I says to him, "it's my opinion there's something queer going on, something that's neither right nor natural. But if there's one man who should know more than what we do it's Job Micklewright. After all," I says, "he walks through the blinking tunnel."

'Job didn't need much prompting to start him off. The very next morning it was, if I remember rightly. The old tunnel was smoking away as usual when out he comes. He climbs straight up into my box, blows out his light, and sits down by my stove a-warming himself, for the weather was sharp. "Cold morning," I says. "Ah," he says, rubbing his hands. "Strikes cold, it does, after being in there." "Why?" I asks. "Is it that warm inside there then, Job? It certainly looks pretty thick. Reckon you must have a job to see your way along." Job said nothing for a while, only looked at me a bit old-fashioned, and went on rubbing his hands. Then he says, quiet like, "I reckon you won't be seeing much more of me, Alf." That surprised me. "Why?" I asks. "Because I've put in for a shift," he says. "I've had enough of this beat." "How's that, Job?" I says. "Don't you fancy that old tunnel?" He looked up sharp at that. "What makes you talk that road?" he asks. "Have you noticed something, too, then?" I nodded my head, and told him what I'd seen, which was little enough really when you come to weigh it up. But Job went all serious over it. "Alf," he says, "I've been a good chapel man all my life, I never touch a drop of liquor, you know that, and you know as I wouldn't tell you the word of a lie. Well, then, I'm telling you, Alf," he says, "as that tunnel's no fit place for a God-fearing man. What you've seen's the least of it. I know no more than you what it may be, but there's something in there that I don't want no more truck with, something I fear worse than the day of judgment. It's bad, and it's getting worse. That's why I'm going to flit. At first I noticed nothing funny except it was a bit on the smoky side and never seemed to clear proper. Then I found it got terrible stuffy and hot in there, especially between two and three shafts. Very dry it is in there, not a wet patch anywhere, and one day when I dodged into a manhole to let a train by, I found the bricks was warm. 'That's a rum do,' I says to myself. Since then the smoke or the fog or whatever it may be has been getting thicker, and maybe it's my fancy or maybe it's not, but it strikes me that there's queer things moving about in it, things I couldn't lay name to even if I could see them proper. And as for the heat, it's proper stifling. Why I could take you in now and you'd find as you couldn't bear your hand on the bricks round about the place I know of. This last couple or three days has been the worst of all, for I've seen lights a-moving and darting about in the smoke, mostly round about the shaft openings, only little ones mind, but kind of flickering like flames, only they don't make no sound, and the heat in there fit to smother you. I've kept it to myself till now, haven't even told the missis, for I thought if I let on, folks would think I was off my head. What it all means, Alf, only the Lord himself knows, all I know is, I've had enough."

'Now I must say, in spite of what I'd seen, I took old Job's yarn with a pinch of salt myself until a couple of nights after, and then I saw something that made me feel that maybe he was right after all. It had just gone dark, and I was walking back home down to Frithdale, when, chancing to look round, I saw there was a light up on the Fell. It was just a kind of a dull glow shining on smoke, like as if the moor was afire somewhere just out of sight over the ridge. But it wasn't the time of year for heather burning – the moor was like a wet sponge – and when I looked again I saw without much doubt that it was coming from the tunnel shaft. Mind you, I wouldn't have cared to stake my oath on it at the time. It was only faint, like, but I didn't like the look of it at all.

'That was the night of February the first, 1897, I can tell you that because it was exactly a fortnight to the night of the Garside disaster, and that's a date I shall never forget as long as I live. I can remember it all as though it were yesterday. It was a terrible rough night, raining heavens hard, and the wind that strong over the moor you could hardly stand against it. I was on the early turn that week, so the missis and I had gone to bed about ten. The next thing I knew was her a-shaking and shaking at my shoulder and calling, "Alf, Alf, wake up, there's summat up." What with the wind roaring and rattling round, it was a job to hear yourself think. "What's up?" I asks, fuddled like. "Look out of the window," she cries out, "there's a fire up on the Fell; summat's up I tell you." Next minute I was pulling on my clothes, for there wasn't any doubt about it this time. Out there in the dark the tunnel shafts were flaming away like ruddy beacons. Just you try to imagine a couple of those old-fashioned iron furnaces flaring out on the top of a mountain at the back of beyond, and you'll maybe understand why the sight put the fear of God into us.

'I set off up to Garside Box just as fast as I could go, and most of the menfolk out of the village after me, for many of them had been wakened by the noise of the storm, and those who hadn't soon got the word. I had a hurricane-lamp with me, but I could hardly see the box for the smoke that was blowing down the cutting from the tunnel. Inside I found Perce Shaw in a terrible taking. His hair was all singed, his face was as white as that wall, and "My God!", or "You can't do nothing", was all he'd say, over and over again. I got through to Ennerthwaite and Highbeck South and found that they'd already had the "section blocked" from Perce. Then I set detonators on the down line, just in case, and went off up to the tunnel. But I couldn't do no good. What with the heat and the smoke I was suffocating before I'd got a hundred yards inside. By the time I'd got back to the box I found that Job Micklewright and some of the others had come up, and that they'd managed to quiet Perce enough to tell us what had happened.

'At half-past midnight, it seems, he took an up goods from Highbeck South Box and a few minutes later got the "entering section". Ten minutes after that he accepted the down night "Mountaineer" from Ennerthwaite. (That was one of our crack trains in those days – night sleeper with mails, first stop Carlisle.) Now it's a bank of one in seventy most of the way up from Highbeck, so it might take a heavy goods quarter of an hour to clear the section, but when the fifteen minutes was up and still no sign of her, Perce began to wonder a bit – Thought she must be steaming bad. Then he caught the sound of the "Mountaineer" beating it up the bank from Ennerthwaite well up to her time, for the wind was set that road, but he didn't see no cause then to hold her up, Highbeck having accepted her. But just as he heard her top the bank and start gathering speed, a great column of smoke came driving down the cutting and he knew that there was something wrong, for there was no question of it being anything but smoke this time. Whatever was up in the tunnel it was too late to hold up the "Mountaineer"; he put his home "on", but she'd already passed the distant and he doubted whether her driver saw it in the smoke. The smoke must have warned him, though, for he thought he heard him shut off and put on the vacuum just as he went into the tunnel. But he was travelling very fast, and he must have been too late. He hoped that the noise he heard, distant like, was only the wind, but running as she was she should have cleared Highbeck South Box in under four minutes, so when the time went by and no "out of section" came through (what he must of felt waiting there for that little bell to ring twice and once!) he sent out the "section blocked", both roads, and went off up the line to see what he could do.

'What exactly happened in that tunnel we never shall know. We couldn't get in for twenty-four hours on account of the heat, and then we found both trains burnt out, and not a mortal soul alive. At the inquiry they reckoned a spark from the goods loco must have set her train afire while she was pulling up the bank through the tunnel. The engine of the "Mountaineer" was derailed. They thought her driver, seeing he couldn't pull up his train in time, had taken the only chance and put on speed hoping to get his train by, but that burning wreckage had fouled his road. Perce got no blame, but then we only told them what we *knew* and not what we *thought*. Perce and I and especially Job Micklewright might have said a lot more than we did, but it wouldn't have done no good, and it might have done us a lot of harm. The three of us got moved from Garside after that – mighty glad we were to go, too – and I've never heard anything queer about the place since.

'Mind you, we talked about it a lot between ourselves. Perce and I reckoned the whole thing was a sort of warning of what was going to happen. But Job, who was a local chap born and bred, he thought different. He said that way back in the old days they had another name for Garside Fell. Holy Mountain they called it, though to my way of thinking "unholy" would have been nearer the mark. When he was a little 'un, it seems the old folks down in Frithdale and round about used to tell queer tales about it. Anyway, Job had some funny idea in his head that there was something in that old mountain that should never have been disturbed, and he reckoned the fire kind of put things right again. Sort of a sacrifice, if you follow my meaning. I can't say I hold with such notions myself, but that's my tale of what the papers called the Garside Fell Disaster, and you can make of it what you like.'

WORLD'S END

I never like sharing a room with a stranger, but there are occasions when one must accept such a contingency with good grace. I was on a walking tour in Pembrokeshire at the time, and on this particular day I had planned to reach the 'Milford Packet' at St Bridget's where I had forwarded most of my belongings. But everything went wrong, weather included. My idea was to follow the old coastguard path along the rim of the cliffs, but I eventually had to abandon it. In places the path had been blocked by subsequent enclosures, while in others it had just disappeared owing to coast erosion. To make matters worse, a thick sea-mist was blowing in, so there was a good chance of falling over the cliff edge. This wasn't a pleasant prospect, as you'll appreciate if you know Pembroke. It's as savage a coast as any in Cornwall, and those cliffs in places must be two hundred feet high. I thought I might be able to make up for lost time by walking below the cliffs and just above the tide line, but when I eventually managed to scramble down I found this was quite impossible. Then I struck inland, but the mist obliterated all landmarks, and I lost my bearings completely in a maze of small fields enclosed by those walls of stone and turf which are characteristic of that part of the country. It was then that I abandoned all hope of reaching St Bridget's, and realized that it was a case of making for the nearest shelter, for it was still early in the year, and to be caught by darkness would have been the last straw. I was just beginning to visualize a comfortless night in some barn or other, when I struck a familiar lane and knew that if I followed it back towards the sea it would bring me to the 'World's End'.

You may perhaps have heard of the 'World's End', for it's quite well known, and all the guide-books mention it. It's a little isolated inn standing four square to the winds on Trevean Head above a little fishing cove of the same name. As you may imagine, it's associated with various tales of smuggling in 'the good old days'. It's a grand place to call for a glass of beer on a fine day, but it did not look particularly cheerful or hospitable to me when I eventually saw it loom up out of the darkness and the mist. Admittedly I was feeling pretty miserable, for I was very cold and my clothes were soaked by the mist and the spindrift which the wind was whipping off the sea.

There was only one room available in the house, a room with two beds in it, one of which was already occupied, but I must say they did their best for me. There was a roaring fire in the little parlour, and they produced a good hot meal and strong tea liberally laced with rum. My room-mate excited my curiosity; he wasn't the type I would ever have expected to find in such a place – not at this season, anyway. He was a shy, little, self-effacing, nondescript fellow; obviously from his speech and appearance, a townsman, and possibly a clerk. I put his age at sixty or over, for his face was wizened and shrunken and his head quite bald. He gave me the impression that his nerves were not all they might have been because his weak eyes were very restless behind his thick-lensed glasses, while he seemed as if he could not keep still, but must be for ever standing up and sitting down, shuffling his feet or making vague fluttering movements with his hands.

The night didn't begin well, for it was a long time before I could get off to sleep. The wind, which had risen almost to gale force, filled the room with draughts, and rattled the ill-fitting door and window. At intervals of a minute or two, the whistling buoy off Trevean Head wailed like a lost soul, while every now and again I could hear a booming noise like the distant sound of heavy gunfire, caused, I imagine, by the heavy sea running into some cavern under the cliffs. And as if this chorus was not sufficient disturbance, my companion kept tossing and fidgeting about in his bed in the most exasperating way. At last, however, I managed to doze off, for I was dead-tired.

I awoke from a curious dream to find that my room-mate had lit the candle which stood on the table between our beds and was pacing up and down the room in his pyjamas. This was the last straw.

'What on earth's the matter?' I called out.

At the sound of my voice he started visibly, paused irresolutely for a moment or two, and then came and sat down on the foot of my bed. I could feel that he was trembling, and the expression of misery in his weak, blue eyes (he had taken his glasses off) was piteous. I couldn't be angry with the wretched little man, so I asked him again, gently this time, what was the matter. He found his voice then, and proceeded to tell me his story. It may not sound much as I tell it to you now, but try to imagine it spoken in a flat, hopeless monotone in that cold, candle-lit room full of the sound of the sea and the hooting of that infernal buoy. Desolate was too good a word for it. I felt as if I really was at the world's end. I can hear his voice now.

'It's thirty years since I last came here, and spent the night in this room,' he began. 'But I knew I should come back one day, sooner or later. I was on a walking holiday then, the same as you are, and they gave me the selfsame bed here that you're in now. I went off to sleep soon enough and then – well, whether I really woke as I thought I did or whether I dreamt it all, I've never rightly been able to tell. Anyway, all of a sudden I found there was a candle burning in the room, on that table there where it is now, and that there was a little old man with a bald head pacing up and down, up and down in front of my bed. I was startled; not just because they hadn't told me there was going to be someone else in my room, but because in some queer sort of way I felt I recognized the old chap, though for the life of me I couldn't place him – not at first, that is. He seemed terribly upset and troubled in his mind about something, and though I don't actually recollect that he spoke to me, yet somehow I knew that he was in pain, that he'd got some awful trouble – incurable – if you know what I mean. And, then – oh, it was horrible, and I couldn't do anything but lie there and watch – he goes over to the table there, takes a revolver out of the drawer and shoots himself through the head. Then everything went dark again.'

By the time he had finished this story he had grown quite hysterical, and I tried to console him, telling him it was only a dream and that it was all a long time ago anyway. But he kept shaking all over and rocking to and fro muttering 'Horrible, horrible', with his head buried in his hands. Then all of a sudden he got up off the bed, crossed over to the dressing-table which stood under the window, and began grimacing at his reflection in the mirror in the most ghastly sort of way. Finally, he turned round and faced me, his face so contorted that it looked scarcely human.

'Don't you see?' he screamed at me. 'Don't you see? It was me that I saw, me as you see me now.'

It was then that I realized that he had a revolver in his hand. He must have taken it out of the little drawer under the mirror. The whole thing had become sheer nightmare, for although I knew quite well what was going to happen next, I just lay there quite powerless and could do nothing to stop him.

Yes, he shot himself right enough. Nor was he under any illusion either, because in the dream I had before this happened, I had seen a man whom I thought I recognized: a man who was blinded and terribly scarred. And that was twenty years before I met with my accident in the blitz of '41.

HEAR NOT MY STEPS

It was a large, gloomy room, and cold. Davies leant from his chair by the hearth and stirred the logs into a blaze. But neither the fire's light, nor that of the candles which flickered and guttered in the draughts from ill-fitting doors and casements, could dispel the shadows from the corners of the panelled walls or from the great four-poster bed with its faded hangings. He got up, and for the fourth time made a thorough examination of the room. He found nothing unusual. The seals he had placed over doors and windows were intact, and no moveable objects had been disturbed from the chalk rings he had drawn round them. His thermograph recorded a slight fall in temperature, but no more than might be expected at the approach of midnight. He returned to his chair, yawned and picked up the book he had been reading. This business of Psychical Research upon which he had embarked so enthusiastically was beginning to pall. In the past two years he had kept similar vigil in four alleged 'haunted rooms' in different parts of the country, from none of which, according to local superstition, he had any right to emerge alive. But no incident which, by any stretch of imagination, could be attributed to supernatural agency had rewarded his patience, discomfort and loss of sleep. It looked as though this, his fifth experiment, was going to prove equally fruitless.

No longer expectant, his eyelids drooped, and he must have dozed, for when he opened his eyes once more and glanced at his wrist-watch, the hands pointed to half-past midnight. He shivered involuntarily, and as he did so he became aware that although the fire still burned brightly, the room had grown very cold. A glance at his thermograph confirmed this sensation, for it had recorded a fall of nearly fifteen degrees since his last examination little more than half an hour before. This was quite abnormal and quickened his flagging interest. He was about to make yet another tour of inspection when his attention was drawn to the shadows beside the bed. They appeared to be moving and thickening in a manner which the flickering of the candles did not explain. As he watched, a pale oval gradually distinguished itself from the gloom, about six feet from the floor. He soon realized that this was a face, and that he was witnessing the materialization of a phantom. At first, the form was very indistinct, but though he heard no sound, it presently began to move, or rather to glide, very slowly away from the bed and towards his chair. As it did so it became clearer, like an image brought into the focus of a glass. He saw that it was the figure of a man clad in a cloak of some drab-coloured stuff which reached almost to his heels. The face was deathly pale, and the dark eyes, opened very wide, stared directly, not so much at him as through him. Davies was not a timid man, and the emotion he felt was one of pity and concern rather than fear. Though it seemed a strange term to apply to a ghost, he thought it was the most haunted face he had ever seen. Terror and misery lurked in the eyes, but otherwise the features were expressionless, a mere mask which the mind within, petrified by some intensity of emotion, could not, and would never again, animate. This impression only lasted a few moments because the figure continued to advance, and as it did so it seemed to lose focus again, becoming once more immaterial and shadowy, until, though Davies thought it might be an illusion of the unsteady light, its shadow seemed to envelop him and to darken the outlines of the room. He glanced quickly behind him, but saw nothing; only his vision still seemed curiously blurred, and try as he would he could see nothing clearly. Even the candle-flames looked indistinct, surrounded by a wavering nimbus of light as though his eyes were veiled by tears.

While he was aware that he had been vouchsafed an experience which most Psychical investigators would envy him, the knowledge somehow failed to arouse in him any enthusiasm. This was due, perhaps, to the defect of vision which troubled him. Gradually, however, he found that his sight was clearing until he could once more see the room quite plainly. Yet still he felt no reassurance; no return of critical interest. Instead, a great weight of undefinable depression seemed suddenly to have descended upon his spirit. Why, he thought, should we mortals struggle to discover what lies beyond the grave when death will come to lift the veil for all of us so soon? What, after all, is the purpose of life, the point of human hopes and fears, ambitions, passions and sorrows? Life is merely a series of distractions which blind us to the one great reality, the reality of death's relentless and unconquerable quest. 'Dust hath closed Helen's eye.' Yes, and worms have long since writhed through that flesh which was once so fair. Since this is my inescapable destiny also, why strive against it, why reject the cool steel of Hamlet's bare bodkin only to suffer the slow corruption of old age?

What could have set him musing in a strain so foreign to his usually cheerful disposition? He put the sombre thoughts from him, struggling to assure himself of a friendly reality like one who wakens from a nightmare. But he found that the task called for an immense effort of willpower. He forced himself to his feet and began, like a man moving in a trance, to examine the room. He could find no trace of any of his seals, and the thermograph had vanished. Yet he could not bring himself to feel any surprise at their disappearance. He had no anticipation of finding them, for they had become the figments of a dream which was rapidly fading from his mind. The room, too, looked subtly different, although here again he could not believe with any conviction that it had ever looked otherwise. The oak of furniture and panelling looked lighter in colour, so did the elm-boarded floor which had lost the wave-like undulations of age. When he looked at the bright hues of the bed-hangings he wondered how he could ever have imagined that they were so old and faded. Somehow, the sight of the bed filled him with an indescribable feeling of loathing and revulsion, so that he moved away hurriedly towards the window and looked out. In his dream (for a dream he was now convinced it was) he had gazed down upon a square of waste land bordered by a row of tall poplars, but now a full moon showed him clearly that there were no poplars, and that the waste land was, in fact, a garden of clipped yews and terraced walks. Had he ever regarded such a prospect with equanimity? Every yew must surely harbour in its grotesque shadow some hostile and malevolent shape, nor was there any solace to be found in the stillness of the night, in the pallid moonlight, or even in the great star-pricked dome of the sky. 'Thou sure and firm-set earth, hear not my steps'; the words of Macbeth echoed in his mind as he experienced a strange feeling of detachment. It was as though the dark globe were spinning beneath his feet, about to cast him out into the desolation of outer space. He gazed up at the sky. What if death were not, after all, an ultimate oblivion, but the prelude to an eternal suspense, lifeless yet deathless, in the cold and dark of illimitable nothingness? His soul shrank from so desolate a conception, and, trembling, he moved back once more into the room. It looked bright in the light of the many tall candles which smoked in their sconces. He understood quite well now that horror lay concealed behind the hangings of the bed, yet an irresistible compulsion drew him there, and before he parted the curtains he knew what he would see.

The woman's hair, fanning out over the pillow's whiteness, gleamed gold in the candlelight. She had been so beautiful, he remembered, whose only glory now lay in this hair. How quickly that beauty had been snuffed out! Where the roses and lilies so lately bloomed, now black corruption already crept. Who would beg a glance from eyes which had started from their sockets to stare so hideously? Or a kiss from lips drawn back to reveal the sharp teeth which had bitten through the protuberant tongue?

On the coverlet lay a length of whipcord. He picked it up, running its taut length between his fingers. Then, very deliberately, he coiled it about his throat and drew it tight. As he did so he realized what he was doing, but his hands continued to strain upon the chord until the sound of choking ceased and it was very still in the room.

AGONY OF FLAME

'I know of an island on a lake in Ireland that would make a more appropriate target for an atomic bomb than Bikini Atoll.'

This unexpected and astonishing statement, and the way in which it was spoken, brought our somewhat inconclusive discussion on the subject of the atomic bomb tests to an abrupt close. It was followed by a few moments of uncomfortable silence during which we eyed the speaker with mingled feelings of embarrassment and curiosity. About forty-five years of age, with hair prematurely white, a sensitive face and the hands of an artist, he was not, judging by appearances and by his previous conversation, the sort of man to advocate the discharge of an atomic bomb anywhere, least of all upon an Irish island. Obviously he read our bewilderment in our faces.

'Oh, yes,' he went on, 'I agree with you all right. I, too, think the bomb should never have been invented, and that it certainly should never have been used. But, on the other hand, I can assure you that if there is one place on earth which should be utterly obliterated it is this island. No, I'm not going to tell you where it is; some of you might be inquisitive, and such curiosity, if acted upon, would be dangerous, in fact it might be deadly dangerous. Ten years ago I spent a night on the island. Since then I have quite forgotten what it is like to sleep dreamlessly.' He laughed, but without mirth. 'But I was lucky; my companion was by no means so fortunate. You want to hear about it? All right, but I shall be surprised if you'll believe it however earnestly I swear that it is true.

'I came to the lake in which the island lies by water. My friend – I'll just call him Jack – and I were cruising round the Irish coast in the thirty-five footer which I had at that time, and, using our auxiliary engine, we found our way up the canalized river which connects the lake with an arm of the sea. There are a great number of these fiord-like inlets in Ireland, particularly along the west coast, so this won't give you much of a clue to our whereabouts.

'It had been what the Irish call a "soft" day, I remember. There was no real weight of rain, but the clouds never cleared the mountains. Sometimes they lifted until they only cut off the high summits, but at times they crept down to water-level and enveloped us in a mist that was deceptively wetting. Though the sky remained overcast the light had that unique silvery, luminous quality which you only find in the west. By the time we reached the lake it was nearly dark. Whistler might have called the scene "Nocturne in Black and Silver", though there was so little colour that it was subject for wood engraver or etcher rather than painter. There was not a breath of wind to flaw the surface of the lake. It reflected so perfectly the last pale light of a sky uncoloured by any sunset that the black shapes of numerous small, wooded islets seemed to float in air, unsubstantial as Prospero's pageant. Once, an arrow-head of wild geese flew honking overhead, and occasionally there floated over the water a raucous sound which I attributed to a heronry on one of the islands. Otherwise, only the steady throb of our little Kelvin engine broke the stillness.

'We Saxons don't understand the Irish, you know, and I don't suppose we ever shall. We label their mysticism "Celtic Twilight" and dismiss it jokingly as a sort of childish whimsy. But if you were to find yourself alone in the west of Ireland in circumstances such as I'm describing, maybe the joke would begin to lose its point. Brought up in a more bracing climate we don't give ourselves time to stop and think, but burn out our lives in an elaborate world of our own artifice. But out there, in the loneliness and the soft, relaxing, misty air, self-importance quickly dissolves, life seems ephemeral, and you begin to understand the Celt a little better; his sense of the past; his lack of ambition which we call shiftlessness; the melancholy that never leaves him even in his joy.

'But I'm wandering from the point. I wanted to convey to you the atmosphere of the place, but unless you have been to the far west yourselves, I think it's beyond my power to do so. Suffice it to say that if someone had assured us that those squawking herons were really Firbolgs or that the geese were the Host of the Sidhe, I am sure we should have believed them. You may therefore suppose that what I am going to tell you is merely the product of a too vivid imagination. In answer, I can only assure you that what follows has nothing whatever to do with Irish mythology, and that it would take more than a Firbolg to turn my hair white overnight.

'I had previously selected an anchorage after a study of my large-scale map – a small bay that appeared to promise good shelter from the south and west if the wind rose. The Irish lakes can be devilish uncomfortable in rough weather. Crossing the lake was rather a tricky business, because we were afraid of rocks and the failing light made visibility very limited. However, we kept going slowly ahead and eventually found our way into the bay without incident. From the little we could see of it, it certainly seemed a snug enough berth, so I put her astern while Jack went for'ard and let the anchor go.

'Commanding the entrance to the bay was a small island with a ruined castle on it. The walls seemed to rise almost sheer out of the water, in fact it was impossible in the dusk to tell where rock ended and masonry began, and when we passed it on our way in I might have mistaken it for a natural crag if I hadn't noticed it previously on the map.

'I went down into the galley and began preparing our supper, while Jack took the dinghy out to lay a night-line. By this time it had fallen quite dark and there was no moon. I was just getting ready to dish up when I heard the creak of oars, and presently the dinghy nudged the side just below the galley port-hole.

'"Take a look at that ruined castle of yours," Jack shouted.

'"Why, what's the matter with it?" I called back, busy with the frying-pan.

'"Well," he answered, "it doesn't seem to be so ruined after all; there are lights in it. See for yourself."

'I put down the pan and looked out through the porthole. He was quite right. Light shone from what appeared to be windows near the base of the keep. I was at once struck by what I can only describe as the peculiar quality of the light. How can I attempt to explain what I mean? It was so unlike anything I had ever seen before that it was impossible to imagine the source of it. Somehow I felt instinctively that it was not produced by any sort of lamp. In colour it more nearly resembled flame, yet it never flickered nor wavered, while in some extraordinary way it conveyed an impression, not of heat, but of coldness. As we watched, I from the port-hole and Jack from the dinghy, a curious thing happened. The light increased in brilliance slowly and absolutely steadily. This may not sound very odd in the telling, but I despair of conveying to you how strange and unnatural was the effect of this *steadily* increasing radiance. As it waxed, the source of light appeared to rise slowly, floating up, it would seem, from floor to floor. First-floor windows appeared, at first dimly, then brilliantly as the light below waned, the process being repeated on the second storey. Then it descended again, all the while gathering to itself more brilliance until, when it reached the ground once more, it had grown almost uncomfortably dazzling. But only for a time. Another odd feature struck me. Instead of casting a normal line of reflection over the water, the light appeared to irradiate the lake all about the island so that it seemed that the castle lay surrounded by a luminous moat. As we watched, first this strange glow upon the water, and then the light itself became veiled as though with mist, growing fainter and redder in hue until both disappeared in a darkness that was absolute.

'Jack made the dinghy fast and clambered aboard.

'"Well," he asked, "what did you make of that performance?"

'"I think it was very odd, indeed," I replied, "but I don't propose to row about the lake in the pitch darkness looking for mysterious lights. I intend to eat my supper while it's hot, and then turn in. The castle can wait till daylight; probably it won't look so odd then."

'When we awoke next morning a westerly breeze was ruffling the water, the sunlight was brilliant and the air as fresh and clear as crystal. The lake seemed to have lost its mystery. The wooded islands now appeared prosaic and substantial enough. So did the castle. It certainly looked as though it might be inhabited, for it presented to us three storeys of casement windows which were obviously of much more recent date than the fabric of the keep. Yet we could see no sign of life; if there were chimneys they were invisible to us, and we could detect no smoke.

'When we had disposed of breakfast we decided to row over to the castle and satisfy our curiosity. We were only half-way to the island when we made our first singular discovery.

'I was rowing, and Jack, sitting in the stern, suddenly said: "Look!" and nodded towards the castle.

'I shipped my oars, looked over my shoulder and saw at once what he meant. The windows we had seen were not, in fact, windows at all, but white, wooden shutters having upon them the painted semblance of frames and sash bars. We looked at each other, then, for a moment, saying nothing, and somehow, in spite of the bright sunlight, the castle no longer seemed quite so prosaic. Then I rowed on.

'We circled the island until we found a ruined stone quay where we were able to run the dinghy in and step ashore. Have you got a feeling for places? I mean, do you find that some places are friendly while others are quite the reverse? Well, I have; and the moment I stepped out of the boat I knew that this island was the most unfriendly spot I had ever been in. Jack was insensitive to impressions of this sort and noticed nothing, but we both remarked the complete lack of life of any sort on the island. It was simply a mass of naked rock and masonry standing up out of the water. There was no grass; there did not even appear to be any moss upon the stones which looked as though they had been blackened by fire. No jackdaws wheeled away as we walked through the arched doorway into the shell of the building; except for the wind and ourselves nothing stirred. I say "shell" because the place had obviously been burnt out. It had no roof, but consisted simply of four stark walls with their sightless window apertures. The destruction had been singularly complete for, with the exception of the window shutters which had obviously been fitted subsequently, there was not a scrap of woodwork left. Only square holes in the masonry remained to reveal the position of the floor joists.

'I am not usually a nervous man, but I must confess that my immediate, instinctive and almost overmastering impulse was to get back to the boat as quickly as possible and push off from the beastly place. Not so Jack. While I waited in growing uneasiness he carried out a methodical and exhaustive examination until he was finally forced to admit that his curiosity was, not satisfied, but completely baffled.

'It was a wonder I did not break the thole pins when I rowed away from the jetty, and it was not until there was a hundred yards of water between us and the island that I began to feel better.

'"Well?" I asked.

'"Must have been an optical illusion," said Jack. "Most likely a fire somewhere on the mainland directly beyond the castle. I don't expect we shall see anything tonight."

'I hoped he was right, because I knew that if the light did appear I should have the greatest difficulty in dissuading him from going over to investigate it. Yet his explanation did not convince me, and I don't believe it convinced him either. I knew that if he persisted in going back to the island I could not let him go alone, and the prospect filled me with a feeling of foreboding that was quite without rational cause. I suggested that afternoon that we might up anchor and move to another part of the lake where the fishing was better, for we had caught nothing on the night-line. Would to God that we had gone! But Jack would have none of it.

'"Why should we?" he asked. "Fishing isn't everything, and we've got a snug berth here. Besides, I want to see whether that light appears again."

'Poor devil, what a price he was to pay for his curiosity!

'When the sun touched the ridge of the mountains I felt my heart sinking with it. The wind had dropped completely and the lake looked indescribably beautiful in the evening light, yet I found myself hating the place, dreading the purple shadows that were thickening under the trees, and wishing myself anywhere but there. As soon as it grew dark, Jack kept peering through the port-hole in the direction of the castle. No light had appeared by the time we had finished our supper. My spirits rose a little and I began to assure myself that I'd been a fool, when Jack looked out once more and this time motioned me to join him. There was still no light in the castle itself, but the water round about the island appeared to have become very faintly luminous.

'"Looks as if that must be the first part of the performance which we missed last night," he said. "Come on, let's go over; we should just have time before the real fun starts."

'I did everything I could to dissuade him, but to no purpose. You couldn't find a more obstinate fellow than Jack when once he'd made up his mind. So we set off together, he filled with eager curiosity and I with nameless fears. Jack rowed this time, while I sat in the stern, and as the dark shape of the keep rose higher and higher as we drew nearer so my spirits fell. At length we reached the perimeter of the luminous water, and as I looked down, little points of light appeared to be moving beneath the surface. Jack momentarily stopped rowing to look down, too.

'"Phosphorescence," he said briefly.

'But I had seen that phenomenon in the tropics, and this did not look the same. The moving lights looked to me – absurd though this must seem to you – more like little tongues of flame. I had chosen Irish poetry for my reading on that trip, and almost before I was aware of it I found myself repeating in my mind a stanza from that queer poem by Yeats called "Byzantium". Know it?

> '"At midnight on the Emperor's pavement flit
> Flames that no faggot feeds, nor steel has lit,
> Nor storm disturbs, flames begotten of flame,
> Where blood-begotten spirits come
> And all complexities of fury leave,
> Dying into a dance,
> An agony of trance,
> An agony of flame that cannot singe a sleeve."

I still think that it was apt.

'The first disaster happened as we came ashore. We put in to the old quay as before. Jack shipped his oars and held on to the stonework while I got out; then he passed me the painter and followed. I was holding the painter with one hand and groping with the other for an old iron ring which I had found that morning, when it was suddenly jerked out of my hand. For an instant I thought it was Jack playing the fool; then I heard a swirl of water and turned just in time to see the faint white shape of the dinghy disappear into the darkness as though borne away on some swift current.

'"My God!" I cried. "The dinghy's gone."

'Jack came back through the darkness to stand at my side.

'"What on earth happened?" he asked.

'I told him, but it was plain that he thought it was merely clumsiness on my part. He was so sure of it that he almost convinced me, and yet with no wind, why should the boat have swung away so fiercely? Lakes don't have currents as a rule.

'"Oh, well," said Jack resignedly, when he had finished twitting me for my carelessness, "we shall just have to make a night of it now, that's all. She may drift back; otherwise one or both of us'll just have to swim for it when the light comes. It's not very far to the shore."

'This was not very reassuring. The island in daylight had been bad enough, but in this darkness the sense of imminent menace was infinitely worse. It would be five hours before the dawn came, and meanwhile there was the possibility of the appearance of another and less friendly light. We did not have long to wait.

'We had been so absorbed by the loss of the dinghy that we had failed to observe the fact that the "phosphorescence" had disappeared from the water, but now we realized that we stood in total darkness. We were groping our way along the quay when Jack suddenly gripped me by the elbow.

'"It's here again,' he whispered in tense excitement. "Look there!"

'I saw it as soon as he did. We were approaching the doorway into the keep at an oblique angle, but we were near enough to see that there shone from it that steady, flame-like light which we had seen the night before. Looking up – and this will seem to you fantastic – we saw that the windows were also luminous. We stopped. The light was dim, but as we watched it grew, and as it grew we became aware of a sound. I think I can best describe it as a sort of hissing, bubbling noise like that of a great cauldron boiling, though that won't give you any idea how horrible it was. At the same time I felt, though this may have been imagination, as though the solid rock was vibrating, ever so slightly, beneath my feet. Quite frankly, I was terrified, and I think even Jack was scared, judging from the way he continued to grip my arm. Both sight and sound suggested heat, yet it was deathly cold and seemed to grow colder as the light and the hissing noise increased. The whole island seemed to have become the power-house of some monstrous sort of energy. People argue that fear of the supernatural is simply fear of the unknown; that as soon as it becomes known and therefore "natural", fear will disappear. I disagree. I believe that there are certain things we cannot or should not know, and I think that the source of this unholy light was one of them. Normally, I have an enquiring, sceptical mind, but my prayer at this moment was that I should not see it. Jack, apparently, thought otherwise.

'The light had followed the same course as before, it had risen to the top storey and was now descending, becoming very brilliant. I think I must have shut my eyes when I realized Jack was no longer holding my arm. It all happened in a moment. I opened my eyes to see him striding towards the doorway. I shouted to him to come back, but it was too late. He had wheeled into the doorway and stopped abruptly, just as though a door had been slammed in his face. I could see him all too clearly in that hellish glare. I heard him give a most awful, whinnying cry, much more like an animal than a human being, and then his head jerked back in an unnatural, mechanical sort of way and he began pushing the air before him with his hands as though fending something off. After what seemed an age, but was probably only a matter of seconds, he turned, came stumbling back, and collapsed at my feet. My one idea was to get as far

away from that doorway as I could. Sheer panic gave me strength, and in
next to no time I had dragged him down to the end of the quay. Yet even
here, things were little better. The rocks below the water flickered with
light that I can only call "cold flame", and the water itself seethed and
bubbled, hissing on the margin, while a mist – I cannot call it steam, for
it was ice cold – rose from it, to swirl and thicken about me.

'I shall never know how I managed to endure the rest of that night, nor
shall I ever forget a detail of it. For the most part, Jack lay still, but every
now and again he would recommence that desolate inarticulate crying,
all the while pushing, pushing something away from him that only he
could see. The mist became dense, and it seemed to my distraught mind
that it was peopled with shapes, formless, yet somehow purposive and
evil, advancing towards the castle and glowing like flame in the reflected
glare. I thought, then, as I still do, that the thing in the castle must be an
Elemental – whatever that may mean – and the possibility that it might
advance upon me, through that doorway whose outline I could still see
through the mist, filled me with an emotion for which terror is much too
mild a word. I remembered reading somewhere that if you do not look at
an Elemental you are safe, so I closed my eyes. But it took every shred of
will-power that was left to me to keep them shut. For it was as though
some malignant force was bent upon undermining my will and so
inducing me to open them. It peopled my mind with obscene creatures
which crawled out of the water and pressed close about me so that I had
to cover my face with my hands and press my fingers to my closed
eyelids.

'But at last I felt the horrors leave me, and the air grow warmer. I
opened my eyes slowly and fearfully to find that the blessed sun had
already cleared the woods on the farther shore. The lightest of breezes
was blowing on to the quay, and only a few yards away our dinghy was
nuzzling her nose between two boulders. I retrieved her and tied her up
at the quay. Then I shook Jack and pointed to the boat. He stared straight
through me as though he were looking into a great distance and grunted.
I shook him again and shouted his name, but he still stared blankly into
space. Finally, I dragged him to his feet and armed him down the quay.
He tripped over a loose stone and I had a job to hold him. It was then
that I realized that he was not only deaf and dumb but blind also.'

He paused, and there seemed to be the shadow of remembered fear in
his eyes.

'Yes,' he concluded, 'if you gave me an atomic bomb I should know
what to destroy. If you can believe me, wouldn't you agree?'

HAWLEY BANK FOUNDRY

Mr George Frimley is a successful Birmingham business man. He is the Managing Director of Herbert Frimley and Company, Ironfounders, of Brookend, and he lives in a desirable detached residence situated conveniently near to the golf-course at Sutton Coldfield. His success is manifested to the world in the shape of an expensive car and an even more expensive wife whose blonde hair is of doubtful authenticity, and whose thirst for gin equals that of her husband for whisky. Their other hobbies are golf and bridge. In short, Mr Frimley exhibits to the world a front of prosperous complacency unshaken by any troublesome doubts that a spark of imagination might have bequeathed to him. His philosophy, if it can be so called, is free-trading liberalism. He inherited this, along with his business, from his father. Both were founded in the nineteenth century. Though still in his early forties, he is already 'Old George' to his friends at the Clubhouse, and to the business cronies with whom he may be seen lunching at the 'Queen's Hotel'. To them, his tall, broad-shouldered figure, with heavy jowled red face and sleek, grey hair, has become an institution, imperturbable as the statues in Victoria Square, reassuring as a healthy bank balance. I think that he is jealous of this reputation, and I believe this to be the reason why he is so reticent about his unsuccessful venture in Shropshire in 1941.

Men of George Frimley's calibre build their own secure little worlds around them like a wall, shutting out perplexity, doubt and the fear of the unknown which lurk without. George Frimley built his wall well. When the planes of the *Luftwaffe* droned over Birmingham, when the sky glowed red with fire and the ground shook with the detonation of high explosive he drove his car back from the office as usual, or donned his warden's helmet and patrolled the street with scarcely a qualm. Even when he drove down to Hillend one windy March morning in 1941 and found that the works of Herbert Frimley and Company had been reduced to a heap of rubble and twisted steel he remained, to all outward appearances, undismayed. Yet when the Hawley Bank project was abandoned five months later, 'Old George' spent a further three months recuperating at Bournemouth before he finally returned to Birmingham, and even so his friends were heard to remark that he was not looking quite his old self.

Hawley Bank lies high above the Severn and almost within the shadow of the Wrekin. It is hard to believe that, where all the might of the *Luftwaffe* had failed, anything in this quiet Shropshire countryside should so effectively succeed in forcing a breach in Mr George Frimley's formidable mental defences. Yet this was the case. He has not yet recovered from this assault upon his complacency. Probably he never will. It is an affront to his self-esteem which he prefers not to discuss. Consequently it is not at all easy to discover from him what actually did happen at Hawley Bank.

George was never a man to let the grass grow under his feet. After a brief survey of his wrecked cupolas and core ovens on that fateful morning he drove to the nearest telephone which would function and put a high priority call through to London. He held important war contracts, and his terse conversation set in motion a complex bureaucratic mechanism of telephone calls and urgent minutes between the War Office, the Ministry of Supply and the Office of Works. As a result it was suggested that Messrs Herbert Frimley and Company should, as a temporary measure, occupy the premises of the defunct Hawley Bank Ironworks in Shropshire. He was assured that local labour would be forthcoming and that billets would be found in the neighbourhood for his 'key men'. Accordingly, one bright, early spring day, George Frimley, accompanied by his Foundry Manager, Arthur Clegg, set off from Birmingham to inspect the Hawley Bank Works, and in a very short time (for George is a fast and capable driver) we may imagine the long, black car crossing the Severn and sweeping up the steep hill beyond. It is easy to visualize the scene; the hanging woods on the hillsides misted with the first tentative buds of spring, cloud shadows sweeping over the broad back of the Wrekin and, far below, the silver stream of Severn threading her narrow gorge. But the pair were too engrossed in their business to notice such things. After thirty years in the trade, there was little that Arthur Clegg did not know about the Midlands iron industry, past or present. Soon after they left Birmingham he had confessed that he had never been to Hawley Bank, but suspected that they would find it 'an awkward, old-fashioned sort of place'. Pressed to give his reasons for this belief, he went on to tell the other all he knew of the history of the Hawley Bank Ironworks. George did not find this recital very encouraging.

They were one of the oldest ironworks in the district, it appeared, having been founded by two brothers, Amos and Josiah Darley, in the eighteenth century. They were pioneers in their day, these brothers; perfecting methods of puddling iron, and smelting it with coke on their Shropshire hill-side while their fellow Ironmasters farther east were still feeding the remnants of the Forest of Wyre into their furnaces and laboriously hammering the excess carbon out of the iron under cumbrous, water-driven tilt hammers. The business had remained in the Darley family for generations, but like many pioneers, they failed to keep abreast of the times and soon lost the initial lead which their ancestors had won. By the 1870s only one furnace remained in blast, and by the turn of the century that, too, went cold, no longer able to compete with larger and more modern plant elsewhere. The Hawley Bank Works became exclusively a jobbing foundry; still a prosperous little business with a good reputation for sound work, but old-fashioned in its methods and no longer a great name in the trade. Such was the inheritance of Josiah IV, seventh and last generation of the Darley family, in 1910.

This last Josiah was, it seems, 'a bit of a character', in fact George Frimley had to cut short his Manager's flow of anecdotes on the subject somewhat brusquely. But not before the picture had emerged of a cantankerous and eccentric old bachelor, living in the past, intensely conservative and equally intensely proud and jealous of the family tradition. Until the end of the First World War, this last Josiah remained in sole control at Hawley Bank, and the relationship existing between him, his works and his workpeople more closely resembled that of a traditional country squire to his estate than an industrialist. It was a wonder that Josiah never married, for there was no other branch of the Darley family to succeed him. Of course there were the usual tales about his having been crossed in love in his youth. However that may be, there can be little doubt that the knowledge that he was the last of his line, and that with his death a link which had survived the whole course of the Industrial Revolution would break, must have preyed upon his mind.

Through the war years the work did well, but by the time peace returned, old Josiah had aged considerably, not only in body but in mind. He was, in fact, nearly eighty and, though still remarkably hale physically, he was subject to mental aberrations and lapses for which 'eccentricity' was now too mild a word. Nevertheless, everyone believed that only death would end Josiah's reign at Hawley Bank, so that there was consternation in the works when, in 1920, he suddenly installed a Manager. Josiah would still potter round his works every day, but from then on he practically ceased to take an active interest in the business.

The history of Druce, the new Manager, appears to have been wrapped in mystery. No one knew where he came from, and Clegg said he had never heard of anyone of that name connected with the trade, at any rate in the Midlands. No less mysterious was the way in which the old man who never left his native Shropshire if he could possibly avoid it, ever got hold of him. In the light of subsequent events it seems more probable that it was Druce who got hold of old Josiah. Certainly this sudden introduction of a stranger to such a position, when there must have been several men in the works who might have filled the post, seems quite out of key with Josiah's character. But wherever Druce may have come from, it would certainly seem that he knew his job. In this respect, at least, he was no impostor. But he was utterly ruthless. In place of the old man's paternal rule, Druce at once introduced at Hawley Bank a new regime that was as coldly efficient as it was impersonal. Whereas under old Josiah the workmen were always men – Harry and Tom and Dick – no matter how roundly he might curse them, they were merely numbers to Druce. Time-honoured methods and routines were swept away, and the old day-work system was replaced by keen piece-work rates. There was nothing novel in this, but it was new to Hawley Bank. Many of the old hands left, and there were new faces in the foundry. Others appealed to old Josiah, but Druce seems to have dominated him no less successfully than the rest of the works, for in face of these deputations he would only curse and wave them away impatiently with his stick. He continued to make his daily circuit of the works, but if he noticed the changes that were taking place, he gave no sign.

Then one day the old man failed to appear. Rumour and conjecture were rife. Some said he was ill, others that he was dead. Both were wrong. Old Josiah had disappeared, and was never seen again. He lived alone, and his housekeeper, who came in daily, was apparently the last person to see him. After she had cleared away his evening meal she had looked into the sitting-room to find out if there was anything he wanted before she went home, and saw him sitting at the fireside. He appeared to be in his usual health and spirits. But investigation showed that his familiar rusty bowler and heavy stick were missing from their accustomed place in the hall, so that he must have gone out again later that night.

Naturally, Josiah's disappearance was a nine days' wonder. Copyholt Mere and five miles of the Severn were dragged, but no trace of him was ever found. Soon there was another topic to keep tongues wagging, for it transpired that the old man had left his property, together with his private fortune, which was not inconsiderable, to Druce upon condition that he changed his name to Darley by deed poll. Naturally, Druce was not loath to comply, but, from the moment of this compliance, luck seemed to desert him.

It is clear that Druce (or Darley, as we must now call him), must have antagonized his workmen. That he was heartily disliked there can be no doubt, and this dislike culminated in a strike in the foundry which even Darley could not break. Instead, he had to import out-of-works from the Black Country. Doubtless it was owing to this unskilled labour that Hawley Bank lost its reputation for good-quality castings, and that there was an extraordinary series of minor accidents in the foundry – moulds going up, probably through the cores not being properly dried, and men burnt. This gave the shop a bad reputation, and there was more labour trouble. This state of affairs culminated in a more than minor accident when a big engine-bed casting blew up suddenly when the pouring had almost been completed, and, as a result, three men were lost in circumstances which Clegg preferred not to describe in detail. There was a sequel to this a few days later when, in the same shop, Darley, alias Druce, was found hanging from the hook of the overhead crane. It was suicide, of course.

So far as is known, no relatives ever came forward, but even had they done so they would have gained very little, for it was found that the Darley fortune had almost ceased to exist, while the works had become a liability. For, apart from its bad reputation, this was the slump year of 1929. Hawley Bank Ironworks were abandoned.

'I expect we shall find,' concluded Clegg, 'that the scrap merchants have had most of the more easily movable plant, but apart from this and twelve years of neglect most likely it'll look much the same as it did when Darley or Druce (whatever you like to call him) left it.'

By the time Clegg had brought his story to a close they had practically reached their destination. Following the directions given to him in the last village they had passed, George Frimley slowed down as he sighted a pair of crumbling brick gate-pillars on his right, and presently swung the car off the road and on to the trackway they guarded. It had been a metalled road, but now it was grass-grown except for a narrow central strip which was evidently still in use as a footpath. But presently even this slender evidence of usage veered sharply away into the woods to leave the track untrodden. The car bounced uncomfortably on the uneven surface, and the long tentacles of encroaching briars clawed at the windows. George was more concerned at the rough treatment his shining car was receiving than by the melancholy history of Hawley Bank Ironworks.

'Blast this bloody war,' he swore. 'Whoever in his right mind would think of trying to start a business in this God-forsaken place? Still, that's the Ministry's concern, not mine. If we can't do the job in Birmingham then there's nothing else for it. At least Jerry won't find us here in a hurry. . . . This road will have to be made up for a start,' he went on, slowing the car to a walking-pace.

Over the tree-tops appeared a tall, square chimney-stack. Even at this distance it was apparent that its old weather-mellowed brickwork was sadly in need of pointing. Halfway up the shaft a small bush had taken root. How many years had passed since last it had smudged the clear air above it with smoke? Smoke is to a chimney as leaves are to a tree, and a derelict stack has always the gaunt, forlorn appearance of a dead tree. A moment more, and the car debouched into a clearing wherein lay the Hawley Bank Ironworks. George stopped the car, and the two men got out. The building nearest to them had obviously been an engine- and boiler-house, for not only did the chimney-stack rise from the end wall, but the nose of an old egg-ended boiler protruded through the masonry. Walking through the doorway (the door itself had disappeared) they discovered a great beam engine. George was tall, but the enormous cylinder towered above him, while overhead in the gloom of the higher galleries, the ponderous beam hung poised at the top of its stroke like some titanic grasshopper petrified when about to spring. A faint, stale smell of cylinder oil still pervaded the building, and from a nail on a wall that had once been whitewashed hung an old and dirty cloth cap meshed over with a fine net of cobwebs. Obviously the engine had been out of use for a considerable time – since the last blast-furnace was shut down, Clegg conjectured, for it was evidently a blowing engine. A student of engineering history would have been deeply interested, but the past meant nothing to George who merely expressed surprise that the engine had not been dismantled for scrap years before. Clegg guessed that old Josiah's eccentricity had spared it during the previous war, while when the works closed in 1929, the price of scrap would not have paid for the cost of dismantling.

They walked out of the engine-house, passed the rusty ruin of the last blast-furnace, and entered the foundry. This was a substantial brick building, and except for the fact that most of the glass in the iron-framed, round-headed windows and in the skylights was broken, it appeared to be in unexpectedly good repair. Doubtless it had been renovated and improved during Druce's brief regime. It consisted of one lofty and capacious bay over the moulding-floor, and two side aisles, one of which housed the cupolas and the other a range of core ovens. One large cupola remained. Clegg tapped its rusty steel side with an iron bar he had found, peered into its throat with the aid of a torch, and expressed the opinion that if it was re-lined it might be put into service.

'Phew!' he added, withdrawing his head. 'Doesn't it stink, though. Dead bird or something must have dropped in from the top.'

Brick foundations and a circular hole in the roof were evidence that a second and smaller cupola had been removed. Some of the core-oven doors were missing and, except for a pile of old wooden patterns, dusty and cracked, all the more readily portable equipment, such as mould-boxes and ladles, had gone. But whoever had dismantled Hawley Bank Works had not considered it worth his while to remove any of the heavier plant. Even the travelling crane still hung overhead. It was of the old manual traversing type and bore upon an oval, cast plate the legend: 'Josiah Darley and Company, Ironfounders, Hawley Bank Works, 1898.'

The two men padded to and fro, their footfalls silenced by the black sand of the moulding-floor which filled the air with a pungent, acrid odour. It was so quiet that when a cloud darkened the sun and the wind stirred and rattled some loose steel sheet on the external charging gallery round the big cupola, both stopped and started involuntarily. Clegg walked across to the small doorway beside the cupola, peered up at the gallery, and then returned, looking rather shamefaced.

'Funny thing,' he said. 'I could have sworn there was someone hanging around outside.'

George grunted, but said nothing.

They continued their examination in silence. A sudden storm of hail beat upon the roof. The noise it made seemed prodigious, and when it ceased as abruptly as it had begun it seemed to leave the stillness the more intense, even though it was now punctuated by the stealthy crepitation of water dripping from broken downspouts and shattered lights. Now it was George's turn to stride suddenly across the foundry to the doorway by the cupola and look out.

'What's up?' called Clegg.

'Nothing,' said George.

'There's someone hanging around outside,' Clegg repeated. 'Some nosey parker from the village, most likely.'

But if this was so, their watcher moved with remarkable stealth and circumspection, betraying himself by neither sight nor sound.

'There's one thing that strikes me as odd about this place,' Clegg went on.

'What's that?' asked the other.

In answer, Clegg pointed with the toe of his shoe to one of the numerous holes which pitted the sandy floor.

'Rats,' said George laconically.

Clegg looked doubtful and wrinkled his brows as he idly kicked sand into the hole and stamped it down with his foot.

'Maybe,' he agreed at length, 'but it's the first time I've ever known rats do that – reckon the sand's too soft and they don't like the smell of it.' He paused. 'Anyway, whatever it is, it could be a nuisance. Better put rat poison down. We need some new sand, too.'

He picked up a handful from the floor, squeezed it in his palm, looked at the cake, impressed with the marks of his fingers, crumbled it and let it fall. The sun came out again, throwing a sharply etched pattern of broken roof-lights on the dark floor. They walked round the outside of the building discussing the structural repairs that would be necessary and the installation of new equipment, together with whatever might be salvaged from the wreckage at Brookend. Though neither man would have entertained such a project in normal circumstances, both agreed that it would be quite feasible to re-open the foundry. As they strolled back to the car, still talking technicalities, the sun was fast setting over Wales. The keen evening air was filled with the scent of decayed leaves from the surrounding woods where, in mist and purple shadow, night was already advancing. The ironworks, too, were now in shadow. Only at the top of the tall chimney-stack did the crumbling brickwork glow red in the last of the sunlight. Wiping his scrupulously polished shoes on the grass, George had a final look round. The prospect apparently gave him no pleasure. He shivered involuntarily, turned up the collar of his opulent camel-hair overcoat, and got into the driving-seat. The starter whirred, the wall of the engine-house echoed the slamming of car doors, and the long, black saloon crept away through the woods.

As the shadows came out of the woods, so stillness and solitude returned to Hawley Bank, and only footprints in the sand of the moulding-floor remained to tell of its interruption. But not for long. As has already been remarked, George Frimley never wasted time. A few days later, two lorries roared up the track through the woods, one carrying a gang of men and the other a light road roller. Soon the track had been re-surfaced with blast-furnace slag cut from the old grass-grown tip. When these pioneers had done their work more lorry loads of men and materials appeared; builders, bricklayers, painters, glaziers and labourers; steel trusses and joists, corrugated sheeting, bricks, sand, bags of cement, gravel. Long-disused paths about the works became muddy tracks between piles of scaffolding, planks and other paraphernalia. All day long the clearing echoed the fussy tuff-tuff-tuff of small engines driving hoists and concrete-mixers. A cupola, salvaged from Brookend Foundry, was installed in place of the missing one, while the highly skilled work of building a new firebrick lining into the big cupola proceeded slowly. The first builder fell sick, had to give up the job, and it was difficult to find anyone to replace him. However, along with the other structural work, the job was eventually completed, and as the builders moved out, Brookend Foundry began to move in; mould-boxes, patterns, modern foundry machines that Hawley Bank had never seen, and, finally, furniture and equipment for the new office building which had been erected near the engine-house. New faces appeared in the surrounding villages; the local bus company arranged special morning and evening services to and from Hawley Bank. The ponderous machine that George Frimley had set in motion that March morning with a telephone call to London had done its work, and Hawley Bank Foundry was re-born. One hot July day, for the first time in twelve years, the mouth of the big cupola belched pungent reddish-tinted smoke. Later, the smoke cleared and only the shimmering sky above the squat, steel cylinder betrayed the intense heat within.

Apart from minor difficulties and excitements, all went well at first. Some of the Birmingham men grumbled at what they called 'a God-forsaken hole', missing their cinemas and pubs and street-corner fish-and-chip shops, but the majority were glad to sleep sound in their beds after nights spent in air-raid shelters. Clegg was worried about the rats in the foundry. In spite of a systematic poisoning campaign and the introduction of new moulding sand on to the floor, the holes continued to appear. They were only a minor irritation so long as they were casting in boxes, but he realized that if ever they had occasion to run a big cast moulded in the floor, the trouble might become serious. He repeatedly complained to George Frimley about it, but George, who was not a practical man and was overwhelmed with administrative work, told him brusquely that he had rats on the brain and that he had better put more water with it.

'Try a couple of cats,' he added facetiously as his office door closed behind his disgruntled Manager.

Strangely enough, Clegg accepted this advice. A few mornings later, much to the amusement of the staff, he arrived in his car accompanied by two lean tom cats which he had procured in the village on the assurance that no rat could live within sight of them. At no little inconvenience, he kept them in the office that day but, having given instructions that all the moulds should be covered to avoid possible damage, the cats were shut in the foundry for the night. Next morning, as soon as he arrived, a grinning foundry foreman came to the office door.

'That chap you got the poison from, Mr Clegg,' he said. 'He must've thought you said cats, not rats.'

'What d'you mean?' snapped Clegg, who was feeling tired and in no mood for jokes.

'Your cats,' said the other, slightly aggrieved at his reception, 'they're dead, both on 'em.'

And sure enough they were. They were also curiously limp, as though every bone was broken through falling from a great height. As Clegg reflected, it was a curious end for one cat to meet, let alone two.

The holes continued to appear in the foundry floor, but Clegg made no more experiments with cats. His absorption with the rat problem was becoming a works' joke, and this made him self-conscious about it. But the thing worried him, and one evening after the moulders had knocked off he went down to the foundry and examined the holes minutely, looking for footmarks or droppings in the soft sand. He found neither, though the sand appeared to be tamped smooth by something at the entrances to the holes. This discovery only perplexed Clegg the more, but he said nothing about it at the time.

The next incident worthy of note was the spy scare. To begin with, this wasn't taken very seriously because the story came from little Tommy Callow, a fifteen-year-old apprentice. Sent on an errand from the foundry to the office he returned almost breathless with excitement claiming that he had seen a spy. Scenting a good opportunity for a leg-pull, the moulders affected to take this announcement very seriously.

'What did 'e look like, Tommy lad?' asked one.

'How d'you know 'e was a spy?' asked another. 'Did 'e say "'eil 'itler" when 'e saw you comen?'

''Corse not,' said Tommy, ''e was a little ole feller in funny cloes, an' I know 'e was a spy 'cos 'e 'ad false whiskers on.'

''Ow could yer tell, Tommy? Did yer pull 'em?'

'No, but I know they was 'cos they was all kind 'o white an' straggly like.'

'Go on, you're thinking of Father Christmas; it 'ent time fer 'im yet.'

'Where was 'e, and where did 'e goo?'

''E was a-lookin' round the side o' the cupaloe, just out there,' said Tommy, pointing to the doorway. 'Then 'e popped 'is 'ead back, an' when I went round to look for 'im, why, 'e'd gorn.'

'Cor!' ejaculated the first moulder, sounding deeply impressed, ''e must've jumped inter the bleedin' cupaloe. Must've bin Ole Nick hisself you sin, not one 'o them Nasties.'

'Go on,' said his mate. 'That was never Ole Nick, that was ole Josh Darley a-hoppin' around, him what they say disappeared and wasn't never seen no more.'

But at this a third moulder, a local man, spoilt the fun.

''Old tha rattle,' he said, giving the last speaker a queer look. 'What dust tha want ter goo puttin' such notions in the kid's yead for?'

There was a moment's awkward pause, and then the little group split up rather sheepishly and went on with their work.

It was when two or three of the moulders claimed to have seen the figure by the cupola that Tommy's story ceased to be regarded as a joke, and the spy scare spread through the works until at length it reached the ears of George Frimley himself. His reaction was typical.

'Damn nonsense,' he retorted. 'We had enough of these tom-fool yarns about spies and fifth column in 1940; don't let me hear any more of it. In any case, who in hell would want to spy on us? There's no secret in cast iron.'

Arthur Clegg agreed. He did not believe the spy story either. On the other hand, he did recall a certain occasion when both he and Frimley had peered out of that doorway by the cupola expecting to see – what? It had been an inquisitive yokel from the village then. Upon reflection, he decided that it might be wiser if he did not ridicule the spy yarn quite so forcibly as Frimly was disposed to do. Some other and more disturbing theory might take its place.

Altogether, Arthur Clegg did not feel happy. He had disliked the place at first sight. The gloomy, deserted buildings with those dripping trees pressing round them on all sides had, to use his own phrase, 'given him the willies'. But this was his job, and had he raised any objection to the move on such vague grounds he knew quite well what George Frimley's response would have been. But now these first vague premonitions appeared to be confirmed; to be taking a tenuous shape which seemed to him to bode trouble. Apart from the 'spy' story he was still worried about the inexplicable holes in the sand of the moulding-floor. Surely this mystery could be solved? If whatever it was that made the holes was never visible in daylight, then it followed that it must be nocturnal. They were not working a night-shift. He resolved to come back to the works the following night in an attempt to settle the matter once and for all.

He stopped his car by the engine-house. It was a still, clear night, but moonless, and the tall, black finger of the chimney-stack was faintly silhouetted against the cold starlight. He was reminded of his first visit, for although it was almost uncannily quiet – not a leaf or twig moving in the woods – he experienced the same sensation of discreet but purposeful surveillance. At that moment he would have given a great deal to be by the fireside in his comfortable billet reading the latest 'who-done-it?', but Mr Arthur Clegg was no coward. Resisting the temptation to jump back into his car, he walked resolutely, torch in hand, towards the foundry. Far away in the east, searchlights suddenly slashed the night sky, wheeling in great tentative arcs for a while before concentrating in a dense pyramid of light.

'Hell!' he swore to himself. 'Give me Jerry sooner than this, any day.' But what exactly there was to be afraid of he could not have said.

When he reached the foundry he switched off his torch, opened the door very gently, and stepped inside. It was pitch dark. It was also quite silent except for the fact that his heart seemed to be thumping like a pile-driver. He knew there were no mould-boxes near the door, so he advanced a few inaudible paces over the sand. Then he stopped again, listening intently. His plan was to wait in darkness until he heard a movement and then shine his torch in the direction of the sound. He stood perfectly motionless for what seemed ten minutes, but was probably not more than two. At length his straining ears caught what he could only describe later as 'a kind of slithering sound'. It was so faint, and the stillness was so intense, that he thought it might merely be caused by some small settling movement of the sand. Also the direction of the sound was indeterminate, it seemed to be everywhere and yet nowhere, so that he did not switch on his torch. The next instant the suspense was terminated in so sudden and shocking a fashion that fifty-year-old Arthur Clegg cried out involuntarily like a man on the point of waking from a nightmare. His left ankle was so abruptly and strongly gripped that he lost his balance and fell heavily, dropping his torch. Through his thin sock he could feel that whatever held him with such crushing force was cold and slimy and that it was moving in what he afterwards called 'a heaving sort of way'. He groped desperately for his torch. As he did so he felt a clammy, tentative touch upon his face, but, fortunately for his reason, upon that instant his fingers found the torch and he switched it on. He had fallen with his head beside one of the holes, but there was nothing to be seen. In the instant of turning on the light, the grip on his ankle had relaxed and, twisting round, he directed the beam in that direction. As he did so he thought he saw something of indeterminate shape and of dirty white colour disappearing into the sand. Clegg scrambled to his feet and was back at his car in a time that did credit to a man of his age and lack of training. When he got to the main road he stopped and smoked a cigarette to steady his nerves. Then he drove home and drank three times his customary tot of whisky before he went to bed. But he did not sleep very well.

He came to the office next morning very shaken and considerably perturbed in mind. The sun shone out of a cloudless sky, birds sang in the woods, and from the works came the familiar and, to him, very comfortable sounds of human activity. His experience of the previous night seemed as remote as an evil dream. Yet he knew very well that it *was* no dream, but that, in the night-time, something nameless, but peculiarly horrible, stalked, or rather crawled abroad in the foundry. His previous vague uneasiness now crystallized into the certainty that some power of malevolent and hostile purpose was fast gathering strength in the ironworks, pressing close about the place like the encircling woods. But what was he to do about it? The premises upon which his conviction was based were so slender. He knew only too well what George Frimley's reaction would be if he attempted to relate to him his experience of the previous night. He would probably lose his job.

A conversation which he had with the foundry foreman later that morning in no way reassured him. As he had feared, the 'spy' rumour was no longer current. It had been superseded by another of an even less credible but more disquieting kind. Through the agency of local gossip in their billets or in the bars of the 'New Invention' and 'The Woodcollier', the men had got hold of the whole story of old Josiah and Druce. They had also been told the usual village yarn that the ironworks was haunted and that no villager would ever go near the place. The actual form of the haunting varied according to the fertility of rural imagination. Druce was to be seen hanging from the crane hook in the foundry. Druce haunted the track through the woods, pacing up and down with his head lolling on one side and his eyes hanging from their sockets. It was not Druce at all, but old Josiah Darley who haunted the place. He had been seen standing in the doorway of the engine-house with a long, white beard down to his knees and his eyes glowing like fiery coals. Against all these versions old Charlie Penrice, one of the 'Woodcollier's' 'regulars', stoutly maintained that it was neither one nor the other that haunted the place but both. Hadn't he seen them with his own eyes one moonlight night chasing each other round and round the foundry, Druce with a bit of rope round his neck, and old Josh hopping after him like a spider?

In the ordinary way, these local yarns, which attach themselves to thousands of deserted buildings, would have been merely amusing. But coupled with the persistent rumours of the unknown someone hanging around the big cupola, they did a lot of harm. True, the reports of those who claimed to have seen this lurking figure did not square with any of these lurid figments. Its eyes did not glow like coals or start from their sockets. It carried no spectral accoutrements of ropes or chains, though no doubt with the passage of time and the exercise of imagination it would acquire such embellishments. For the present it remained just 'somebody', and no one had yet succeeded in enlarging or elaborating upon young Tommy's original description of 'a little ole feller in funny cloes' with whiskers 'kind o' white an' straggly like'. Some did not see this much; some saw nothing, but said they felt he was there; others were never aware of anything at all. But Tommy's 'little ole feller' had ceased to be a joke in the foundry. There was an uneasy atmosphere in the shop which effectually set at naught the Government exhortations for 'Maximum Production' which screamed from the posters on the walls. The men were nervy, there was no mistake about it, and it was probably this which was the cause of a number of minor accidents, burns or crushed fingers. But to the men it was proof of their conviction that there was no luck about the place. It was noticeable, too, that they always used the main doors at each end of the central bay, and that the side door by the big cupola was kept permanently bolted upon the inside. It was lucky that the two men whose job it was to charge the big cupola were not numbered among those who claimed to have seen or felt the presence of the stranger, othewise work in the foundry might well have suffered more positive interruption.

These facts only increased poor Clegg's perplexity. Things were becoming serious. Output was affected, and it was obviously his duty to report the whole matter to George Frimley even though he dreaded the consequences. He was still trying to make up his mind that afternoon when the question was solved for him by a message to the effect that he was wanted at once in Frimley's office.

'Sit down and take a look at this,' said George, as he entered. He slid across the desk a blue-print headed 'Dulchester Machine Tool Co.'

'New tool-up for the Achilles engine,' George explained succinctly, 'body casting for a new type of multi-spindle borer. Twelve off to begin with, probably more to follow if the job's satisfactory; 1A Priority. Think we can tackle it?'

Clegg pondered the drawing for a few moments before replying. It was a straightforward casting, and the coring would be simple. The only difficulty was its size. He estimated its weight as little short of three tons. He knew that this was well within the capacity of the big cupola and that they had a three-ton ladle. The electric crane which they had introduced in place of the old manual one could swing this load. But he also knew, and with the realization came an inexplicable sense of impending calamity, that he had no mould-boxes large enough. In fact, with a large, simple casting of this description the obvious course was to sink the mould in the floor of the shop.

'Well?' asked George impatiently, drumming with his fingers on the highly polished desk-top. 'What about it?'

'We could tackle it, all right,' Clegg answered reluctantly, 'only trouble is we have no mould-boxes big enough.' Before the words were out of his mouth he knew what the answer would be.

'Mould-boxes!' stormed the other. 'Mould-boxes! Who wants mould-boxes? Damn it, you're the practical man, not me; what do I pay you for? Cast on the floor, man; even I know that much. Do I have to sit here to teach you your business?'

George's anger roused poor Clegg to the pitch of desperation, and almost before he was truly aware of what he was doing he had blurted out the whole story beginning with the rat poison and the cats and ending with his own nocturnal experience. He also mentioned the stories which were circulating in the foundry. His halting narration was punctuated by a series of grunts and snorts from his impatient listener whose colour was mounting ominously. At length it was brought to a sudden conclusion as George Frimley struck the desk with such force that a little spurt of ink shot up from the ink-well to stain the virgin white of the blotting-pad.

'Am I running a works or a bloody mad-house?' he shouted, the veins bulging in his forehead. 'First of all it's spies, and now it's some damn fool nonsense about ghosts started by a pack of country yokels with nothing better to think about. As for you, Clegg, it's supposed to be your job to knock some sense into these idiots and get some output from them, instead of which you're worse than the lot of 'em put together – you and your bloody rat-holes! If there was no war on and I could replace you, I'd pack you off to a home for inebriates. Now,' he concluded in a quieter voice, 'let's get down to the job and hear no more of this damned nonsense.'

But Arthur Clegg, though subdued, was still resolute. 'Very good, Mr Frimley,' he agreed, 'but I would like to make one stipulation.'

'All right,' said the other, somewhat mollified and impressed by his quiet tone. 'What is it?'

'I cannot agree to accept all responsibility for anything that may happen on this job,' said Clegg, his hand on the blue-print before him. 'All I ask is that you should be present in the foundry when we run the first cast.'

George Frimley grunted. 'All right,' he agreed grudgingly. 'All right, my time's precious, but if it will put a stop to all this infernal drivel it will be worth it.'

Upon this understanding, preparatory work on the big castings was put in hand. Photostat copies of the drawing were taken; the job was priced; a wooden pattern was made and delivered to the foundry by the pattern makers in smooth, snugly fitting sections painted glossy black and red. Soon the first mould was taking shape in the sandy floor. Things seemed to be settling down. Whatever it was that tunnelled the moulding-floor seemed to have suspended its activities. The lurking figure by the cupola had not been seen for some time, and the men began to use the side door again. Even Arthur Clegg's fears were lulled into a sense of security. None the less, he was still obstinately determined that George Frimley should be present when the time came to run the first of the big casts.

Sure enough, at four o'clock in the afternoon of a sultry August day, George duly appeared in the foundry. Everything was ready. The blower hummed steadily, and its fierce blast roared in the molten heart of the big cupola. Its steel sides radiated an intense heat that smote the face with an almost physical force. Before its mouth stood the three-ton ladle ready coupled to the overhead crane.

'O.K.?' queried the foundry foreman.

'O.K.' nodded Clegg, standing beside Frimley, and the orderly routine began.

The furnace-man drove his long rod through the fireclay stopping in the furnace mouth, there was a scintillating flicker of sparks, and the molten metal gushed into the ladle. As he stood waiting with his plummet rod to stop the flow, a black silhouette against the glare, his shadow, vastly magnified, wavered on the opposite wall. There were some who said afterwards that they saw there also a second and shorter shadow. Whether they did or no can never be determined. Certainly there was no one beside him at the time, and the illusion quickly vanished as the man plugged his furnace. There was a whirr of motors overhead as the crane lifted and swung the ladle across the shop towards the mould. The furnace-man knocked over the switch of the blower motor, and the steady hum deepened and gradually died away, leaving the shop strangely silent. The foreman signalled with the palm of his hand to the crane-driver, and the ladle was gently lowered into position beside the mouth of the mould. Two men manned the hand-wheels which would tip the ladle, a third held a skimmer to keep the dross from entering the mould, while a fourth prepared to take out the stops and to light the gas as it issued from the mould vents. Their faces, running with sweat, gleamed in the glow of the molten metal which dimmed the daylight of the roof-lights overhead. The silence of this rather tense moment was broken by an unexpected sound. Somebody laughed. It seemed to come from the direction of the big cupola. Everyone, George Frimley included, glanced in that direction, but the furnace-man was sluicing his face in a bucket of water in the far corner of the shop, and there was no one there. Clegg knew very well that it was not the furnace-man, for the voice was too thin and cracked. It was, he said, more a kind of snigger than a laugh.

The interruption was only momentary, for molten metal cannot be kept waiting or it becomes too glutinous to pour. The stops were taken out, the pourers swung their handwheels, and the mould began to fill. The vents ignited with a 'plop' like a gas-ring and showed flickering blue tongues of flame. Judging by the contents which remained in the ladle, the mould should have been three parts full when the ghastly and inexplicable thing happened.

The black sandy floor just behind the mould suddenly bellied upwards as though moved by an earthquake and, with a sound like a gigantic roman candle discharging its ball of coloured fire, a fountain of molten metal shot high into the air. There was an urgent shout of 'Hey up!' and everyone scattered. The wretched skimmer was caught in the deadly hail and stumbled towards the doorway, screaming like a woman, his clothes reduced to smoking rags. One of the pourers tripped over a mould-box, fell, and did not rise again. There was a sickly smell of burnt flesh. But for the moment the survivors had no eyes for the victims. In the hole which had opened in the sand a pool of molten ore seethed and bubbled angrily. Upon it, or within it (for in some strange way the metal appeared to have become translucent) they saw, what they all agreed to be a corpse. What or who it had been no one can say, for not only was it burned beyond hope of recognition, but it was also in the last stages of decomposition. Around it, seemingly impervious to the fiery element in which they moved, crawled creatures of most sickening shape. They resembled maggots seething and writhing in putrid flesh except for the fact that they were the size of a man's forearm.

*   *   *

Clegg retired prematurely from the foundry trade and now lives in a small cottage near Henley-in-Arden where he grows tomatoes and keeps bees.

Apart from the fact that he never paid a nocturnal visit to Hawley

Bank Foundry, George Frimley was made of sterner stuff. But, as you already know, he spent the next three months recuperating at Bournemouth. But he is still a changed man. For one thing he is not so readily given to shouting at his employees, and his golf handicap is not what it used to be.

As for Hawley Bank Ironworks, even in these days of Scrap Metal Drives, much of the plant still lies there. The big beam engine still lurks in the ruinous engine-house like a great grasshopper eternally poised to spring. But George Frimley's business is back in a rebuilt Brookend, and there is no new tenant. Winter gales have stripped tiles from the roofs; water drips again from choked and broken guttering. The old silence has fallen once more in the clearing of the woods. Even the grass is creeping back over the newly made road and the tendrils of the briars will soon meet across the way.

MUSIC HATH CHARMS

When James Heneage rang up one morning in a state of great excitement with the news that he had just inherited the property of Trevarthen in Cornwall, and to suggest a joint visit of inspection, Thornton accepted the proposal with alacrity. He had known James well since their schooldays, and they shared many tastes in common. Moreover, the fine spring weather made the prospect of exchanging the streets of London for the Cornish cliffs particularly attractive. The house was said to be furnished and, assuming it fulfilled his expectations and that he could obtain suitable domestic help, James expressed his intention of occupying it, at any rate for the summer months. As he was at that time engaged upon a study of the early Celtic civilization of Cornwall, which involved considerable local research, such an arrangement would suit him admirably. They arranged to meet the following morning beneath the clock on No. 1 platform at Paddington. Meanwhile, in a mood of pleasurable anticipation, Thornton looked up Trevarthen in Morrow's *Guide to Cornwall*, and found the following brief entry:–

> TREVARTHEN HOUSE AND COVE (Map 2, Sq. 6c). Small but picturesque private fishing cove in Mounts Bay. Penzance 10 m.; Helton 6 m. Traditionally associated with activities of Count Hennezè, notorious eighteenth-century smuggler and wrecker. Rugged cliff scenery.

As it would be difficult to find a Cornish cove which did not boast 'rugged cliff scenery', and which was not popularly associated with smuggling in fact or fiction, this information left Thornton little the wiser.

James Heneage had never visited Trevarthen, and at the time that he received the news of this unexpected legacy from an uncle whom he had not seen since early childhood, he knew no more about the place than Thornton. His sources of information, however, were not confined to Morrow's *Guide*, for his library included a comprehensive collection of historical and topographical works on the Duchy, including the great Borlaise, and these, as may readily be imagined, he had lost no time in consulting.

The next day, while the Cornish Riviera Express bore them swiftly into the West Country, he imparted the fruits of this research to Thornton, with the result that by the time they had rumbled across Brunel's great bridge over the Tamar, the latter felt that he was already well acquainted with Trevarthen.

The house stood on the shoulder of Carn Zawn Head, its windows looking across the gulf of Trevarthen Cove towards the arc of Mounts Bay. It was a massive building of Cornish freestone of indeterminate date which was believed to occupy the site, or to incorporate portions, of two previous dwellings. In fact, one authority advanced the theory that the first building at Trevarthen was a Celtic 'dun' or cliff fortress similar to King Arthur's Castle at Tintagel. This, however, was purely speculative, for the recorded history of the place began with the Trevarthen family. Minor Cornish gentry who held the estate for many generations and played only a small part in the great events of their day, their history seems to have been in no way remarkable. The last of the line, Sir Peter Trevarthen, supported the Royalist cause in the west, and when that cause foundered with the fall of St Michael's Mount his estates were confiscated and broken up. Before the Restoration which might have recouped the family fortunes, he had died impoverished, embittered and without an heir. Thereafter a curtain of obscurity falls upon Trevarthen House which does not lift for a hundred years. Either it stood empty or, as seems more probable, it was partly occupied as a farm-house. But in 1750, the curtain rises upon a melodramatic scene, for in that year Count Hennezè acquired the property and there began a brief regime which made the name of Trevarthen notorious throughout Cornwall.

Count Pierre Hennezè du Hou, to give him his full title, is said to have been of Huguenot family and to have come to Cornwall by way of the Channel Islands, but no more is known of his past history or of the reason why he chose to establish himself in this remote and, by this time, semi-derelict house. That he was a man of substance we may gather from the fact that he brought with him his own retinue of ten servants. He was also accompanied by a lady reputed to be his mistress, but who was euphemistically entitled 'La Pucelle'.

Among the nobility of the eighteenth century, the practice of vice was a fashionable pastime, while the average Cornishman of those days feared neither God nor man. But the Count seems to have triumphantly overcome this initial handicap to found a reputation second to none. Tales of unlimited licence and debauchery spread abroad, and needless to say he was reputed to have sold his soul to the devil and to dice regularly with this obliging fiend. No doubt such tales were deliberately fostered by the Count and his bunch of thugs (for they must have been little better) in order to deter inquisitive strangers. In this they seem to have been successful, for although coastguards and preventive men must have been aware of what was going on, they apparently made no serious attempt to interfere with the landing of cargoes of contraband in Trevarthen Cove. An even more lucrative source of revenue were the wrecks on the Goat Reef. The Count was reputed to lure vessels to their doom on the Goat by showing a false light on Carn Zawn Head, but these stories of wrecking by means of false lights usually have little foundation. When the great gales lashed the seas to fury round that savage coast those pitiless shark's teeth of rock must have done their work often enough without such aids. Even in these days of steam and diesel power they still claim their victims. False lights or no, there were an unprecedented number of wrecks on the Goat during the Count's regime, and we may imagine that the few survivors met with little mercy at Trevarthen.

As is so often the case, a reign of violence ended in violence. A local fisherman laying lobster pots off-shore noticed that both the house and the cove seemed deserted and that the Count's lugger was missing from her usual berth. Emboldened by this unusual stillness he brought his boat into the little harbour and landed at the quay. Under the cliffs where the zigzag path descends from the house he found the body of Count Pierre Hennezè du Hou with contorted face and broken neck. But of the rest of his gang, including 'La Pucelle', there was no trace. The superstitious declared that the devil had claimed his own, but the more reasonable explanation which found favour with the majority was that 'La Pucelle' had become jealous and persuaded the others to murder the Count before making off with as much of his ill-gotten gains as they could lay their hands on.

'Quite a colourful story,' concluded James with a laugh. 'Good enough for a schoolboy thriller, don't you think?'

Thornton nodded. 'What happened to the house after that?' he asked.

'Oh, nothing of any interest,' answered the other. 'It stood empty again for many years until my great-grandfather took it, and apparently spent a lot of money in doing it up. Funnily enough,' he added, 'he's supposed to have been of Huguenot descent, too, though he didn't take after the wicked Count. By all accounts he was highly respectable.'

Thereafter the conversation drifted to more general topics until the train slid down the long incline from St Erth and they saw they majestic shape of St Michael's Mount framed in the carriage window. From Penzance station they took a bus, alighting from it at the point where the narrow lane which descended to Trevarthen Cove made junction with the main road. It was a perfect spring evening, still and cloudless, the air soft as only Cornish air can be. The main road had taken them out of sight and sound of the sea into bleak uplands punctuated by the gaunt, stone chimney-shafts of derelict tin-mines, but as they followed the lane downward the uplands unfolded to reveal blue water, at first only a pool prisoned by the great arm of Carn Zawn, but presently stretching away to the horizon. And soon they scented the salt tang of the sea, and heard again the eternal voice of the Cornish coast; the endlessly recurring thud and surge of the waves against the cliffs of Trevarthen, and the lost crying of the gulls. At the foot of the hill, the track veered to the left, skirting the lip of the cove, and it was here that Heneage and Thornton first caught sight of Trevarthen House, a long, low building of weathered stone sheltering beneath the arc of the headland. Its windows, facing westwards over the sea, glowed with reflected fire from the setting sun. For a few moments they stood entranced by this romantic spectacle before pressing on up the farther slope towards the house. James almost ran in his eagerness to set foot in his new home.

'I quite forgot to tell you,' he panted over his shoulder to Thornton, who was doing his best to keep up with him. 'There's an old couple – name of Penrice – who are supposed to be looking after the place. I sent them a wire, so they should be expecting us.'

They reached the low, arched doorway, pulled an iron ring which jangled a bell somewhere in the back regions of the house, and Mrs Penrice duly appeared. She proved to be a voluble old lady, so it would be tedious to recount the conversation which ensued. But if she was garrulous she was also efficient. She had prepared beds for them; an appetising and highly seasoned aroma which suggested Cornish pasty wafted out from the kitchen, while the way in which she directed her docile husband to relieve them of their suitcases left little doubt as to who was in control of the establishment. First impressions of the house seemed to justify their highest expectations, but as darkness was falling, and as they were tired and hungry after their journey they decided to postpone any detailed tour of inspection until the morning. After they had consumed Mrs Penrice's pasty, which convinced James that he need look no farther for domestic help, they sat for a while in the flickering firelight of the low-ceilinged dining-room before retiring contentedly to bed. The sound of the sea soon lulled them to sleep.

Thornton never slept with drawn curtains, and when he awoke after a dreamless night the sun had already cleared the rim of the headland behind the house and its light was streaming into his room. He lay for a while in drowsy content before he got up, dressed, and walked out on to the narrow front terrace where James presently joined him. The morning promised a continuance of the fine weather, for the shape of the Mount across the bay was blue and indistinct and the sea was calm. Both men were in high good humour, and after they had consumed an excellent breakfast they commenced a thorough exploration of the house.

It was not, as James had feared, too large; four good bedrooms, excluding the servants' quarters, and on the ground floor three large and well-proportioned rooms in addition to the usual domestic offices. With the exception of a few good examples of an earlier epoch, fittings, furniture and decoration reflected a deplorable mid-Victorian taste. But James was undismayed, declaring that the house possessed infinite possibilities, and as he paced to and fro excitedly formulating his plans, Thornton began to visualize how readily Trevarthen would respond to his friend's good taste.

They agreed at once that the drawing-room to the south of the west front was potentially the most attractive room in the house. Though it boasted three large windows, two set in deep embrasures with window-seats facing west over the sea and a third facing south, it was at present darkened by massive mahogany furniture quite unsuited to its proportions, and by a hideous wallpaper of repetitive floral pattern.

'I shall make this my library and work-room,' James declared, dismissing the furniture with a wave of the hand. 'Just imagine,' he went on, 'all this junk cleared away and the walls cream colour washed.'

'Yes,' the other agreed, 'but you'll have to strip this paper off before you can colour wash, if I know anything about old houses it's probably about fifteen layers thick.'

As he said this, Thornton was idly smoothing the surface of the wall to the left of the fireplace with the palm of his hand. In doing so he made a discovery that he was afterwards destined most bitterly to regret. His fingers detected and followed a slight symmetrical irregularity in the surface of the wall beneath the paper. He felt, and then felt again.

'I say,' he asked eagerly, 'got a knife on you?'

'Yes,' said James, coming across the room and taking out a pocket-knife. 'Why?'

Thornton took the knife and opened the blade. 'Unless I'm much mistaken,' he answered, 'there's a cupboard behind here. Mind if I cut the paper?'

'Not a bit,' James assured him, and added with a laugh, 'perhaps it's full of the old Count's loot.'

After a few moments probing, Thornton made a neat rectangular cut in the paper which was interrupted only in three places by what were undoubtedly the hinges and latch of a door. The next thing to do was to open it. After layer upon layer of paper had been peeled off, it became obvious that the cupboard was not locked, but was held by an inside latch the lever of which had been removed and the resulting hole plugged up. To push up the latch with the aid of a strong kitchen knife obtained from Mrs Penrice was the work of a moment. The door opened to reveal a small cupboard of three shelves let into the thickness of the wall, but to their unbounded disappointment it appeared at first glance to be empty.

'Wait a minute, though,' said Thornton, stooping to peer into the dark lower shelf. 'What's this?' He thrust in his arm and dragged into the light an oblong wooden box about the size of the average deed-box. It was beautifully made of oak with elegant brass mounts.

'Aha!' exclaimed James exultantly. 'The treasure. What's the betting? Diamonds, doubloons or only the missing will?'

They carried it into the light and set it down on the table by the window. The lid opened quite easily. And then after their high expectations both men burst out laughing at the incongruous nature of their discovery. For it was a musical box.

Closer inspection, however, revealed that this was no ordinary musical box. It operated upon the normal barrel-and-pin principle, in this case the barrel being of wood studded with brass pins. But instead of striking the usual comb, these pins opened the valves of a set of little organ-pipes which were supplied with air by a diminutive bellows worked from the barrel spindle by a crude form of cam action. The barrel was rotated externally by a neat S-shaped handle which was at present detached and lying snugly in a compartment at the side of the case. It was, in fact, a miniature version of those 'barrel organs' which were widely introduced into village churches towards the end of the eighteenth century.

Most musical boxes exhibit, on the inside of the lid, a list of the tunes which they play, but in this case there appeared a contemporary engraving in mezzotint which occupied the whole surface of the lid and which was even more remarkable than the instrument itself.

It depicted, with remarkable vigour and detail, a scene of shipwreck. Under an ominous sky and amid mountainous seas a tall three-masted vessel was rapidly breaking up on the rocks beneath towering cliffs. Small figures could be seen clinging desperately to the rigging. Hovering in a lowering cloud in the extreme left-hand top corner of the picture a flying figure directed from inflated cheeks a blast of air upon the sails of the doomed ship in that convention beloved of the early cartographers. But scrutiny revealed that here was no curly-headed, dimpled cherub, but a creature of so unpleasant and menacing an aspect that Thornton quickly turned his attention to the foreground. But here the artist's singular and grotesque imagination was displayed with equally skilful and disquieting effect. Upon a narrow strip of beach out of reach of the waves, a group of figures, seen in black silhouette, appeared to be dancing before a fire. Finally, upon the cliff-top directly above were two more figures. Of these, one was a tall man who stood at gaze, apparently dispassionately regarding the scene below. The other, a shorter figure, stood, or rather crouched, close beside him. The artist had not accorded this last figure the same precision of treatment and attention to detail which characterized the rest of his work. Its vague and shadowy outline failed to suggest a human shape, yet after careful examination Thornton came to the conclusion that if he were to be confronted with a choice of two such evils he would rather encounter the monster of the air than this creature on the cliff. The engraving was unsigned, but along the margin was an inscription the significance of which Thornton could not comprehend. It ran: *HAR, HAR, HOU, HOU, danse ici, danse là, joue ici, joue là.*

'Well, what do you make of it?' asked James, who had been leaning over his shoulder during this examination.

Thornton raised his eyes from the picture and looked out over the calm sea beyond the window for a few moments before replyling. 'I think,' he answered slowly, 'that it's a most unpleasant thing. I don't profess to understand what it all means, but if you'll take my advice you'll pitch it over the cliff.'

James looked at him in astonishment. 'My dear fellow!' he expostulated. 'What on earth makes you talk like that? Anyone would think it was an infernal machine. Damn it, man, it's only a child's musical box and a very rare one at that from the look of it. We've made a find here, and I wouldn't dream of throwing it away.'

'Have it your own way, then,' said the other, with a shrug of the shoulders. 'Perhaps I'm being a fool. But,' he added, 'I would hardly describe it as a toy. That pretty picture on the lid would give most children the horrors.' Thornton paced across the room to the fireplace while James again bent over the musical box.

'It's certainly in rather queer taste,' he admitted. As he said this he took out the little curved handle and fitted it over the barrel.

Thornton heard the faint click as it went home and turned to see what he was doing. Without knowing what prompted him to do so he cried out: 'For God's sake leave the thing alone!' But James only laughed and turned the handle.

At first the instrument only produced a sibilant noise, not unlike the eager panting of an excited dog; then suddenly it broke into a shrill piping tune to the rhythm of a lively jig. But it was like no tune that Thornton had ever heard before. It reached a top note that, like the squeak of a bat, was almost beyond the range of audibility and whose piercing quality positively hurt the ear-drum. The tune rose to this thin yet deafening climax, or fell away again in a series of exuberant capriccios quite horrible to hear because the dissonance of their diminished intervals never seemed to find resolution. Again, despite the comparatively small volume of sound it produced, the instrument seemed to possess the power to awake sympathetic resonance, not only in the table upon which it stood, but in surrounding objects, until the whole room seemed to be whistling in unison.

Thornton, who thought he had never heard so hideous a sound, eventually found he could stand it no longer and shouted out: 'For heaven's sake, stop that fiendish din!'

Obediently, James stopped, withdrew the handle, replaced it carefully in its compartment, and closed the lid. He was smiling in a curious, sly sort of way.

'Why?' he asked. 'Don't you like it? Perhaps I've got no ear for music, but personally I think it's rather fun.' He tucked the box carefully under his arm and moved towards the door.

'Well, I think it's horrible,' said Thornton bluntly. 'Where are you going with it, anyway?'

'I'm taking it up to my room,' the other answered. 'I'm not going to give you the chance to smash my musical box when I'm not looking.'

'I wish to hell I could,' Thornton muttered as James disappeared up the stairs.

In a brief half-hour the wretched thing seemed not only to have raised a barrier of mistrust between them but to have emptied the house of all content. The happiness of yesterday, and even the pleasure and excitement of the morning already seemed to have receded into a remote past. With difficulty, Thornton tried to analyse his feelings. It was as though they had somehow awakened Trevarthen House from sleep, and that this wakefulness was hostile. He realized that he hated the place and was filled with an urgent desire to get away from it as soon as possible.

As he could give no valid reasons for this impression, Thornton hesitated to mention it to James, who appeared to be insensitive to any such change of atmosphere. For the rest of the evening he seemed in high good humour and continued eagerly to discuss his proposed alterations. Yet although it may have been imagination, Thornton thought he could detect a certain forced quality about James's gaiety, a certain nervous restlessness which had not been noticeable the previous evening. He thought, too, that Mrs Penrice seemed to be ill at ease and to look strangely at his host while she was serving dinner.

Thornton slept badly that night. To begin with, the weather broke unexpectedly, the wind veering to the south-west and rising to a gale which was accompanied by lashing squalls of rain. Though his room was on the landward side, he could hear, above the tumult of the wind, the thunder of heavy seas breaking upon the rocks. On its exposed site, Trevarthen caught the full force of the gale so that the house seemed full of sound. Casements rattled, there were minor creaking noises which suggested stealthy movement, and once a door slammed somewhere. At one time he awakened from an uneasy doze and thought he could hear faintly the eldritch sound of the musical box, but decided that it must be the piping of the wind. Once, too, he thought he heard James talking, or rather calling out, in his sleep.

By the time dawn broke, a grey, reluctant dawn of flying cloud, Thornton had finally resolved to leave the place as quickly as he conveniently could. James came down late. He looked pale and distracted and yet, in a queer sort of way, rather smug, as though he nursed a secret joke. In response to his friend's enquiry he protested that he had slept well, though Thornton noticed that he seemed reluctant to look him straight in the face. The barrier of reserve which had come between them now seemed to have grown insurmountable, yet Thornton doubted his ability to excuse his premature departure convincingly. It was a measure of the change which had come over their relationship that he found it necessary, on the pretext of posting an urgent letter, to send himself a telegram from the post office in the neighbouring village. It arrived while they were at lunch.

Though he made polite protestations of disappointment at the news of his friend's imminent departure, James made no attempt to dissuade him; in fact, Thornton thought he seemed secretly relieved. He even helped to speed his parting guest by looking up time-tables.

'There's a bus from the corner,' he announced, 'which connects with the eight-forty night sleeper from Penzance. That'll get you into Town in time for your appointment in the morning.'

That evening, as he stood on the doorstep bidding good-bye to his host, Thornton's conscience smote him at the thought of his precipitate desertion. While nothing would have induced him to change his mind, he felt guilty and uneasy at the thought of leaving James alone at Trevarthen; but, illogical though it was, this feeling of uneasiness could be associated with nothing more tangible than a musical box.

'I know you think I'm a fool,' he said diffidently, as he took James's hand, 'but do take my advice and get rid of that musical box; I couldn't tell you why, but I just don't like it.'

But it was no use. James only laughed. 'Nonsense, my dear chap!' he exclaimed, and then quoted mockingly, '"*HAR, HAR, HOU, HOU, danse ici, danse là, joue ici, joue là*"' As he did so he executed a little capering dance on the doorstep in time with the words, and then giggled.

Thornton did not appreciate the joke. 'Good-bye,' he said abruptly, and turned on his heel.

'Come and see me again when I've finished my alterations,' the other called after him as he walked off through the dusk.

Then the door closed.

The months slipped by and Thornton received no further invitation to visit Trevarthen House; not that he would have felt inclined to accept it, if he had. For a while he continued to feel concern for his friend, but in time he tended to dismiss the cause of this concern as so much imagination. Finally, other preoccupations drove the memory of James Heneage and Trevarthen House out of his thoughts. Or nearly so, for the unprecedented storms of the next two winters brought Press reports of wrecks on the Goat Reef, and this reminded him of James who, he thought, must be having an exciting time.

Three years passed before, one summer's evening, we again find Thornton descending the lane to Trevarthen Cove. Business had brought him to Cornwall and, remembering James Heneage, his curiosity had got the better of him. He drove out from Penzance, but as the weather was fine he decided to leave his car at the crossroads and walk to the house as on the previous occasion. Everything recalled the keen anticipation of that first arrival; the sound of the sea in crescendo as he descended the hill, the cliffs of Carn Zawn, and there, as he turned the corner, Trevarthen House. As he approached the door he realized that his previous impression, which he now most vividly recalled, had not been due merely to imagination. Why he knew this it is difficult to say, but his instinctive impulse was turn back the way he had come, so that to advance to the door and pull the iron bell-ring called for a considerable effort of will. His summons was answered, not by the reassuring figure of Mrs Penrice, but by a soft-footed and obsequious manservant who ushered him into the room where he had made his discovery.

'The master will be with you in a few moments, sir,' he said, speaking with a slightly foreign accent and with a curious emphasis upon the word 'master'.

Thornton looked round the room. James had certainly transformed it, though his taste seemed to have altered considerably. In earlier days he had shared with Thornton a preference for what might be described as comfortable simplicity. But the taste that had furnished this room could only be described as opulent. Or was 'sensuous' a better word? Walls, fitted bookcases, and the deep pile carpet were of a pale greyish-green colour, which was certainly an admirable foil for the rose velvet coverings of the luxurious sofas and chairs and the magnificent brocade window-curtains. One corner of the room was occupied by a grand piano. The cupboard beside the fireplace which he had discovered had been converted into small embrasure. The door had been taken off, the interior painted in a shade of colour slightly darker than the walls and cleverly illuminated by concealed strip lighting. In it reposed the only article in the room which he recognized – the musical box. It was highly polished, and the brass mounts gleamed in the light. The blazing fire made the room almost uncomfortably warm, while there was a faint, cloying scent in the air not unlike incense or perhaps some sort of potpourri.

As is the way with book-lovers, Thornton ran his eye along the bookshelves to discover that James's literary taste had changed no less markedly. He noticed the works of the Marquis de Sade and De Lancre, Glanvil's *Sadducismus Triumphatus*, Sinclair's *Satan's Invisible World Discovered* and various other obscure works of which he had never heard, bearing such titles as *Demoniality* or *Eleau des Demons et Sorciers*. He turned for relief to the walls, but found there evidence of an equally unhealthy preoccupation: reproductions of engravings by Albrecht Dürer, including the celebrated 'The Knight, Death and Satan'; the 'Temptations' of Hieronymus Bosch; a small painting by Fuselli, and a drawing of Beardsley's from *Under the Hill*. On the wall between the windows which faced the sea hung a single painting in oils of the surrealist school. At the first quick glance it appeared to be an ordinary seascape; an expanse of sea stretching to the horizon with rocks in the foreground. But closer inspection revealed that these rocks were of strange shape. In fact, Thornton began to doubt whether the huddled forms upon the beach were rocks at all. He was examining this picture intently and was rapidly forming the conclusion that it was probably the most unpleasant thing in the room, when someone chuckled softly, and he swung round to discover that James had come noiselessly into the room and was standing close behind him. He had grown paler and thinner since he had last seen him, and his eyes were very restless.

'Hullo, Thornton,' he said, extending his hand; 'Glad to see you. What do you think of it?' he went on nodding towards the picture. 'Don't you think it's rather nice? It's a bit of La Pucelle's work.'

'La Pucelle,' Thornton repeated, mystified, and the other laughed.

'Oh, that's only her nickname. Just my little joke in the tradition of the house. Her real name is Jeanne. You'll meet her in a few moments.' While he was speaking Thornton noticed that his friend had acquired some peculiar nervous mannerisms of speech and gesture. At the same time, however, there was something smug and self-satisfied about him as though he still harboured some secret joke. Yet James seemed genuinely pleased to see him. 'I *am* glad you came,' he averred with apparent sincerity. 'Sit down and have a drink. Sherry? You'll stay to dinner, of course.' He took a heavy cut-glass decanter and two glasses from the shelf below the bookcase.

'My word,' said Thornton, as he sipped his drink, 'where did you get this? I can't buy sherry like this in London.'

The other giggled and looked sly. 'You shouldn't ask such questions in Cornwall,' he admonished. 'But, as a matter of fact, I'll tell you. We have to thank the Goat Reef for this. You may have read in the papers last winter about the wreck of the *Santa Maria*. She was bound from Portugal to Dublin, but she got blown hopelessly off her course. A good many of the barrels were broached, but we managed to save quite a few. Sounds like the good old smuggling days, doesn't it? But when you live on the Cornish coast you soon learn to keep a sharp eye on the beach.' He giggled again, rubbing his hands one over the other. 'Oh, yes! I'm quite deeply indebted to the Goat Reef.'

Thornton did not care for the way he said this, and there was an awkward pause which was broken by the opening of the door.

'Here's Jeanne,' James exclaimed, and the two men stood up. 'Jeanne, this is an old friend of mine, Tom Thornton.'

The girl, who was standing on the threshold of the room, inclined her head and smiled. She was tall and of a pale but perfect complexion which contrasted strikingly with a pair of unusually large dark eyes and the mass of black curls which clustered closely about her head. She wore an elegant long-skirted dress which suggested the style of the Second Empire, and as she advanced towards him, moving with superb grace and assurance, Thornton thought she was the most striking woman he had ever seen. Striking, and yet in some indefinable way repellent. He realized that she bore an almost uncanny resemblance to the woman in Fuselli's evil little painting which hung behind his chair. She was doing her best to put him at his ease; talking in a soft, low-pitched, slightly husky voice and emphasizing her words with expressive movements of the hands which seemed to belie her perfect English. But she only partly succeeded, for her hands absorbed most of Thornton's attention. He found himself gazing at them in much the same way as a rabbit stares at a stoat. They were exceptionally long-fingered, and they were bare except for one large and curiously wrought intaglio ring which winked in the firelight. The almond-shaped nails were lacquered the colour of blood. Her presence seemed to heighten the oppressive atmosphere of the room, and Thornton felt mightily relieved when a gong summoned them to dinner.

It was an excellent meal, efficiently served by the same soft-footed manservant who had admitted him, but Thornton did not enjoy it. His host and hostess made themselves very agreeable, but their talk somehow seemed to have that forced quality of adults speaking to a child, while the glances which he intercepted suggested that they shared a life of which he knew nothing. He felt no desire to be enlightened. At one period during the meal there was an interruption. Something, a large dog presumably, snuffed and scratched at the door. James called out sharply some unintelligible word and there was silence.

Afterwards, as they sat over coffee and liqueurs in the library, James suggested that Jeanne should play for them. She complied readily and, seating herself at the grand piano, she began to play softly some slow, sensuous piece which Thornton could not identify, but which reminded him strongly of Debussy's 'L'Après midi d'un Faune'. It was obvious that she was an extremely competent pianist, yet Thornton decided that he liked her playing even less than her painting. While the voluptuous langour of the music seduced his senses there was yet some nightmare quality about it which revolted his reason. Like everything else in that house, it was beastly, and that, he thought, was the only word for it. It was not merely that James had become a voluptuary. That he could easily understand and excuse, even though he might regret it. Intuition told him that it was something much worse than that. He suddenly knew that he could not bear to stay a moment longer. He got to his feet, apologizing for his rudeness and muttering something about having no key to his hotel.

As the front door closed behind him and he felt the cool night air in his face he experienced an indescribable sense of relief. He set off at a brisk pace, resolved that nothing would induce him to visit Trevarthen again. But when he reached the corner he turned to take a last look at the house. As he did so, the front door opened and a figure, which he recognized to be that of James, was sharply silhouetted against the rectangle of light. He seemed to be peering out as though looking for something or someone. And then he saw, dimly visible in the light from the windows, that this unknown someone was in fact moving to meet him. Something about its shape and the way it crouched was very familiar to Thornton, and he confesses that at this point he turned and ran, nor did he stop running until he reached his car.

THE SHOUTING

I companioned Edward on many walking tours before I discovered that he had a positive phobia about woods. There was always some very good reason why we should not go through one: the obvious path, though marked on the Ordnance Survey map, might peter out or turn in the wrong direction; if it was hot there would be too many flies in the wood; if it was evening it would be too dark; half the fun of walking was the view and obviously there could be no view in a wood.

But at last there came a day when none of these pretexts could avail him. On the contrary: it was quite obvious to us, both from the map and from the lie of the land, that to avoid going through this particular wood (which was quite a small one, incidentally) would involve a needless and lengthy cross-country detour including scrambling through many hedges – just the kind of point-to-point walking that does not appeal to me. On the other hand, it was perfectly clear from the stile at the edge of the wood and the path beyond it that there lay a well-used right of way. Yet Edward stopped in his tracks and, knowing there was no valid excuse left to him, said, with an unmistakable fear in his eyes, 'I'd rather not go through that wood if you don't mind.'

'Come on,' I said, 'it's only about a quarter of a mile wide judging from the map, and if we leave the path we're in for a hell of a scramble.' Seeing that he still hesitated, I mounted the stile with a 'Well, suit yourself, I know which way I'm going' over my shoulder. I think it was the nearest we ever came to a row in all our time together.

What followed was really very odd, and cast an entirely new and strange light on my friend. It's odd how long you can know people and yet suddenly discover that you know so little.

Edward padded silently behind me, his eyes darting to right and left as though that harmless Herefordshire coppice harboured every species of savage beast, with the odd poisonous snake thrown in for good measure. But it was no laughing matter at the time, and I confess that I felt a shade uneasy myself, for it was quite obvious that Edward was terrified almost out of his wits.

I was determined to get to the bottom of this unreasoning terror, and that evening in the Scudamore Arms at Combercombe I tackled him about it.

'I'm sorry I persuaded you to walk through that spinney with me. Honestly, if I'd realised that you felt so strongly about . . .'

He cut me short. 'Yes. The truth is that all woods scare me stiff.'

'*My mother said I never should play with the gipsies in the wood,*' I quoted at him rather tactlessly.

Edward gave me a curiously searching look. 'What made you say that?' he asked sharply. Then he went on, 'This has nothing whatever to do with cautionary nursery jingles of that kind. It's due to something that happened to me only ten years ago, just before I met up with you in fact.' And then it all came out.

He was staying in an isolated rented cottage in the bottom of one of those deep and narrow valleys that run down to the Atlantic coast of North Devon and Cornwall. The ridges between them end in formidable bare headlands and vertiginous cliffs that jut out to meet the challenge of Atlantic rollers, but one does not have to go far inland from the coast before their lower slopes are thickly covered with dense woods of scrub oaks, their tops combed by the prevailing south-westerlies that funnel up the valleys till they resemble a smooth green fleece.

Well, Edward said he was lolling in a deck-chair outside his cottage door and enjoying the hot sunshine of late July, when he suddenly heard the patter of feet and the chatter of children approaching down the lane. This surprised him, as there was no village within miles, but when he saw them he thought they must be children of gipsies who had camped nearby, for they were all olive-complexioned with black hair and sloe eyes. They were chattering eagerly together as though anticipating some rare treat, but for the life of him he could not distinguish a word they said. Could they be speaking Ròmany? he asked himself. Surely not.

A boy, who looked about fourteen and appeared to be the eldest and the ringleader of the group, was in front, and as they passed opposite his cottage gate, Edward got up from his chair, stopped the little party and asked their leader where they were going. Speaking in perfect English the boy replied, 'Oh, we are going up into the woods for the shouting.' The way he said this implied that Edward ought to have known the answer without having to ask. But before he could betray his ignorance by asking what he meant, the boy had broken into a trot and the others, silent now but still radiating a tense expectancy, followed him. Edward watched them cross the little wooden footbridge over the stream and then mount the slope until they disappeared into the wood. Then he went back to his deck-chair pondering on this odd little encounter until he began to doze again.

He was roused by what he described as a most unearthly racket: a shrill eldritch piping and shrieking rising every now and again to a frenzied pitch. So this was 'the shouting'. It struck him as a scarcely human sound, sometimes reminding him of the squealing of slaughtered pigs and sometimes of the strange cries he had once heard coming from a heronry. But what puzzled and disturbed him even more was that this shrill clamour seemed to have an accompanying ground bass, a kind of plain chant that was somehow far more horrible to hear – and at this point Edward became almost alarmingly emphatic – than the shouting itself. There could be no one in that party of children with a voice like that, he speculated; it must be an acoustic trick, something like the sound of the sea beating on the rocks at the end of the valley, unnaturally echoed and magnified in that narrow space between the hanging woods. So he rationalised his fear, knowing in his heart that such an explanation could not be true.

It was some time before the children came back: long enough for the sun to have left the floor of the valley, although it still shone brilliantly upon the higher slopes above. They walked silently, two by two, over the wooden footbridge and past Edward's gate with never a sideways glance. He might not have been there, leaning over the gate watching them, he said. Soft-footed, they passed him by as though they were entranced, their lips slightly parted, their sloe eyes staring fixedly ahead as though focused upon some remote distance. Young though the children were, Edward admitted he found this strange procession very awe-inspiring.

He had sat on for a while in the deepening shadow before at length curiosity got the better of him, and he set off towards the wood in the direction the children had taken. He had noticed the spot where the children had entered the wood, for it was marked by a single ancient and stunted yew tree which contrasted darkly against the green foliage of the oaks and their silvery, lichen-bearded trunks and branches. Once he had climbed the fence and entered the woods he found no path, although the way was still clear to him because the children had beaten down briars, nettles and bracken in their passing. Taller than they, he had to walk bent double to avoid the dense interlacement of branches. It was like walking through some low green tunnel. Suddenly, however, he could stand upright, for he found himself in a small round clearing in the midst of the wood. He thought it strange that it was not visible from below, considering the steepness of the slope, which had left him out of breath.

In the centre of the clearing was a low mound of short green turf, like an island in a pool of bracken. Edward walked on to the top of this central mound, and it was at once obvious that it was here that 'the shouting' had taken place. Children were great traditionalists, he reflected; it was doubtless some old country game or ritual handed on by one generation to another.

'*My mother said I never should play with the gipsies in the wood.*' That silly jingle came into his head unbidden and refused to be banished. Evidently they did not forbid such play in these parts, but positively encouraged it. He laughed aloud at this feeble joke; and then he started at the most remarkable echo. Of course, woods were famous for this kind of thing, he thought, but then something much more remarkable and alarming happened: the laugh was repeated from a different part of the clearing.

This time it was no echo but a sound such as he had never made in his life; a deep, short sound, half bark, half bray, human and yet inhuman. The laugh came again almost the next instant, menacing this time, and from the opposite side of the clearing, although he had heard no sound of movement in the wood. At this Edward became terrified. He stood rooted to the spot, peering, now this way, now that, into the darkening wood in an attempt to locate the source of such a dreadful sound.

When the laugh came a fourth time, it happened to sound from the precise direction in which he was peering. It may only have been some trick of the failing light, he admitted apologetically, but an inchoate mass of twigs and oak leaves seemed suddenly to form itself into a gigantic head: a head with an aureole of leafy twigs in place of hair, and a beard of grey lichen below a cruelly smiling mouth. There also appeared to be two red eyes, though this may have been the effect of the setting sun shining through chinks in the leafy canopy of the wood. But, on reflection, Edward thought not. It strikes him now as a last desperate attempt on the part of his rational mind to explain in known terms the unknown. The next instant, sheer panic seized him, and he blundered out of the clearing and down through the wood.

Trees, nettles, bracken and briars all seemed to conspire together to prevent his headlong flight. He nearly scalped himself on low branches, nettles stung him, briars whipped at his clothes and flesh, and tough bracken stalks tripped him so that more than once he sprawled headlong. And all the while that awful voice accompanied him, laughing and chuckling over his plight. He thought that if again he should see the face from which it came his reason would snap. Nor could he bear much longer the sound of that voice and, in a vain attempt to drown it, he began to yell at the top of his voice the first ridiculous words that entered into his head. '*Mother said I never should play with the gipsies in the wood,*' he screamed hysterically.

By the time he finally flung himself over the fence at the edge of the wood his clothes were in tatters and blood was streaming down his forehead and into his eyes from the lacerations on his head. But the horror had left him and, thankfully, he flung himself down on the cool turf, which was now slightly damp with dew. There below him was the dim shape of his cottage beyond the stream, and he gazed at it as a traveller from the desert gazes at an oasis.

'And that was that,' concluded my friend, 'Now you know why I dislike – no, dislike is too mild a word – why I *hate* woods.'

'But what about those children?' I queried, 'Did you . . . ?'

He answered my question before I had finished as, with a shrug of the shoulders, he replied, 'No. There were no gipsies in the district at the time. I made sure of that, and I am equally certain they weren't local children either.' After a pause he went on, 'I asked the good lady from Mortford, who came every day on her bike to do the chores for me, whether there was any legend or traditional custom connected with that particular piece of woodland. But all she would say was "I dunno, sir, us do never goo in ther".'

So your guess is as good as mine as to who or what the children were. Personally, now that I have heard Edward's story, I am inclined to think they may have been the most frightening thing about the whole strange business.

THE HOUSE OF VENGEANCE

The bus from Hereford came to a stop in the somnolent square of the little Welsh border town. The sliding door clashed open and John Hardy, shouldering his haversack, followed two plump and basket-laden farmers' wives on to the pavement. It was a perfect spring afternoon: sunlight drenched the square and, as the clatter of the bus died away along the road towards Brecon, the town's rudely-interrupted peace was quickly restored. The cracked bell in the Victorian clock tower chimed twice. Three-thirty: he would have to step it out, thought John, if he was to make the Priory Hotel at Llanvethney before darkness fell.

He was quite unfamiliar with this Welsh border country, but his friend Alan Brett had explained to him that the hotel where they had arranged to meet and stay lay in a long and narrow valley on the other side of the Black Mountains. Alan knew these mountains like the back of his hand, and had enthused to John so often about them that he had finally persuaded his friend to join him at the Priory Hotel for a week's walking holiday so that he could become more closely acquainted with their beauties. Because Alan had assured him he was fully equipped, John had not bothered to acquire any large-scale maps of the area. But he did not anticipate any difficulty in finding his way, as a preliminary glance at his one small-scale map had shown a bridle road that led out of the little town, over a high mountain pass, and so down into the head of the valley in which their rendezvous was situated.

Walking briskly, he had soon cleared the outskirts of the old town – it was little larger than a village, anyway – and set his face towards the encircling hills. He had done a great deal of walking in the Cumberland Fells and the Pennines and thought that, by contrast, the prospect before him, though pleasing enough, looked rather tame. Surely these gentle hills could not be the wild mountains that Alan had praised so highly. He had covered about five miles, however, when the way veered sharply to his right and began to climb steeply up the flank of a deep and narrow gorge. It was when he had climbed to the head of this gorge that he realised that the hills were merely so many stepping stones to the greater heights which they had hitherto effectually concealed.

A very different prospect now greeted him. He found himself upon the edge of a huge plateau of unenclosed upland, an expanse of short,

springy turf tufted here and there with uncurling bracken fronds and
starred with hundreds of sheep. From this plateau there rose majestically
along the southern skyline the great gables of a range of mountains. A
confirmed 'mountainy' man, John found this prospect very much more
to his liking, and he strode out with a will along the track which he
could see climbing ahead of him round the knees of the mountains in the
direction of the head of the pass.

Meanwhile the range of the Brecon Beacons in the middle distance,
which normally appeared blue and remote, had become darkly
threatening, its outline sharply etched against a great wall of storm cloud
which was rolling up the western sky behind them. Had he not been so
intrigued with the new prospect and better acquainted with the vagaries
of the Welsh border country, so experienced a walker could scarcely have
failed to notice so obvious a threat of impending weather change.

When he had climbed to the head of the pass, he saw that the track
swung away to his left to enter a narrow defile between two mountain
bluffs. For a few moments John thought that the reason why it suddenly
seemed to have become so dark and chilly was that the further of these
two bluffs obscured the westering sun, throwing the pass into deep
shadow. In fact, this dark flank of the mountain concealed from him the
swiftly advancing storm wrack which had already swallowed up the sun.

It was just at this moment when he stood upon the threshold of the
pass that, as it seemed suddenly to grow dark so, as suddenly, he was
seized by a wholly irrational and almost overmastering fear. John was not
a timid, nor even a particularly imaginative, man, and in all his long
experience of walking in lonely places he had experienced nothing like
it. It had to do with something which awaited him on the other side of
the pass. It was as if something monstrous lurked there, and it required a
conscious effort of will to resist the temptation to fly back to the
remembered landscape he had left behind. The weather itself might have
been in league with his unreasoning fears, for as he pressed stubbornly
forward through the narrow defile the whole character of the evening
seemed to change. It became difficult to believe in that sunlit square
where he had alighted not three hours before. The sky had become
totally overcast and every vestige of colour had drained out of the
landscape, to leave it as sombre as the sky. A sudden chill wind, driving a
scud of rain before it, blew through the pass into his face as through some
draughty corridor in which a distant door has been thrown open. This
forced him to lower his head, and when he raised it again he found
himself looking down into the head of the valley.

What he saw did nothing to assuage his misgivings. He thought he had
never seen a more forbidding prospect. He might, he thought, have been
looking down into the dolorous pit of some vast abandoned quarry. The

tops of the mountains that enclosed the valley were already hidden beneath curtains of hurrying cloud, but so steep were their slopes that all he could see of them were a succession of desolate screes surmounted by frowning crags and precipices already dark with rain. The clouds were rapidly coming down; already coils of white vapour were beginning to spiral among the higher crags. A sudden clatter of falling stones on the scree immediately to his right made him start, and he looked up in time to see what looked like a bundle of wool come bouncing out of the mist and over the crags until it slid to rest on the screes below, where it lay very still. It was some time before the stones of the scree adjusted themselves by stealthy crepitation, and it became quite still once more. How typical of this appalling place, he thought, that the only evidence of life should be the death of a sheep!

He began hurriedly to extract a waterproof cape from his haversack, and had hardly got it on before the storm broke in sudden and almost unbelievable fury. The rain lashed down, stinging his face as he blundered almost sightlessly down the track. So dark and lowering was the sky that at this rate, he reflected ruefully, it would very soon be pitch dark, and he cursed himself as he realised that he had brought no torch. Not only had darkness fallen surprisingly early due to the sudden change in the weather, but he realised now that he had grossly underestimated the distance involved. He guessed that Llanvethney must still be at least six miles further down the valley.

The storm had now become a positive cloudburst which no protective clothing could possibly keep out. Cold rivulets found their way down his neck, and even his stout boots were soon squelching. In this wet misery he began to doubt if he could possibly succeed in reaching his destination that night. Had not Alan once mentioned a Youth Hostel somewhere between the head of the pass and the floor of the valley? If so it would make a good emergency port in the storm, if only he could find it. Unfortunately, he had no idea on which side of the track the Hostel lay; nor, as yet, could he see a single light in the fast-gathering darkness.

At last, however, John sighted away to his left beneath the invisible mountain wall a single light shining out, and so wet and lost and wretched was he by this time that he instantly determined to make a beeline for it whether it was the Youth Hostel or not. Surely even the dourest of Welsh hill farmers would scarcely refuse him shelter on such a night. He could just distinguish a gate to the left of the track and through this he passed, plunging down a steep slope in the direction of that solitary light. As he did so he remembered too late that this was the side of the valley which had the stream at its foot and, sure enough, he soon heard above the steady roar of the rain the chuckling of a mountain torrent in sudden spate. Yet still the light lured him on so, somehow or other, he managed to slip and slide down the steep bank, to wade knee-deep through the boulder-strewn bed of the stream and to scramble on all fours up the muddy slope opposite. There were other unseen hazards to be surmounted, such as old thorn hedges and sheep fences topped with strands of barbed wire, before he finally found himself standing on a rough farm track, terraced along the slope, which obviously led in the direction of the light.

A few moments later John Hardy was knocking at the door of the farmhouse. The light streamed out from a curtained window to the left of the door, its fellow on the opposite side being in darkness. There was a sound from within of hob-nailed boots scuffing on flagstones, followed by the rattle of door-bolts being withdrawn. The next instant he found himself confronting a very strange little figure indeed, whose face was thrown into high relief by the light of the paraffin lamp which he held before him, and who peered over it into the streaming darkness. He was so dark-skinned and dark-haired that he might have been a true Romany, yet so short in stature as to be almost a dwarf. He stared disconcertingly at John with unblinking eyes that were black as sloes, and seemed furtive and filled with suspicion. He spoke very rapidly in a sing-song, lilting tongue that John did not recognise. This struck him as very strange because, although he had no command of the Welsh language, he had heard it spoken often enough. Also, he had understood from Alan that Welsh was no longer spoken in this part of the border, so that it struck him as odd that this strange little man, if he was indeed speaking some archaic form of Welsh, apparently knew no second language. However, plastered as he was in red mud and with water running out of his boots, John needed no words to express his plight and so, somewhat grudgingly, the little man stepped back and motioned him to enter. He did not lead the way into the lighted room from which he had obviously emerged, but opened a low dark doorway on the opposite side of the stone-flagged central passage. Signalling the other to follow him, he led the way into a typical small Welsh farm parlour, setting the lamp down on the circular central table.

John would have greatly preferred the homely warmth of the farm kitchen which, as he fondly supposed, lay on the opposite side of the passage. Seen in the dim light of a single lamp, this typical Victorian parlour looked sombre and unwelcoming to a degree and, needless to say, there was no fire in the black and highly-polished grate. He also thought it curious that, in his dripping and muddy state, he should be shown straight into the 'best parlour'. There must, he concluded, be some very good reason why he was not to be allowed to share in whatever was going on across the passage. Nevertheless, he reflected philosophically, at least he had a roof over his head, which was something on such a night.

As soon as he had set down the lamp, his host had straightway left the room, closing the door firmly behind him as though he had other and more urgent business to attend to. Left alone, John removed his cape and his sodden boots and stockings, laying them down beside his haversack in the empty firegrate, before selecting the least uncomfortable looking of the Victorian chairs and settling down to make the best of such cold comfort. He could still hear the steady roar of the rain outside.

Chill and unwelcoming though the room was, particularly to such a damp and benighted traveller, John must have fallen asleep from sheer fatigue, for he awoke with a start, subconsciously aware that some new sound had aroused him. Glancing down at his wristwatch he saw that it was just after midnight. He sat motionless, listening. The buffeting of the storm seemed to have ceased, and in its place he thought he could hear a very unusual sound indeed, which seemed to come from that lighted room across the passage. It resembled, he said, a kind of monotonous chant, although it was quite unlike any form of chant he had ever heard before. It seemed to have a primitive wildness about it, although he could not have explained why he thought this, except that one voice was clearly distinguishable from the others by its curious timbre, which he described as a cross between a rasping chuckle and the bleating of a large goat. Although under the circumstances it was a disquieting sound to hear, he was not particularly frightened. It was what happened next that caused the hairs on the back of his neck to stir.

First of all there was the sound of what John took to be the back door being flung violently open and then slammed to again with a thunderous crash. Instantly the murmur of voices ceased as though that mysterious company held their breath in fearful suspense. For a full minute the house was wrapped in a tense, expectant silence; then there came the sound of earth-shaking footfalls pacing down the flagged hallway. It was, John recalled, as though some ancient and gigantic stone statue had suddenly been endowed with terrible life and was stalking through the house. He remembers staring at the door of the room and praying that it would not open, and that this monstrous thing would pass it by. Loud and startling as a trumpet blast a great voice suddenly cried out: 'Fear not me, fear what follows me.' Then John heard the front door open and slam shut with a violence that shook the house, and all fell silent once more.

It was at this juncture that, with what strikes him now as an inexplicable act of courage or foolhardiness, John opened the casement window of his room and gazed out into the night, although it was pitch dark and he does not recall what precisely he expected to see or hear. Some shadow or sound of that huge presence which had just left the house? Or some presage of that greater fear to come which it had prophesied? At first he could hear nothing except the steady, sullen drip of water from eave to downspout, but then his ears detected a curious sound in the air, seemingly coming from directly above the house. At first it was as if some great flock of migrant birds was wheeling overhead in the darkness, whistling and piping like so many lost souls. The sound gradually grew in volume, however, and as it did so it became loud with menace, an eldritch screaming very terrible to hear. Now it was as though there blew over – or out of – those sheer mountain walls that hemmed in the valley a great wind of such force that the very crevices of the crags and the stones of invisible screes became its vocal chords, screaming and yelling in a unison of violence, 'Fear what follows me.' And now indeed, as he freely admits, John became terror-stricken. There was something so utterly monstrous about this sudden crescendo of tumult in the high air: it was like no storm he had ever known. It was as if the mountains themselves had transformed or perverted a natural element into some tremendous diabolical force.

John shut the window, and as he stood rocking on his feet in the centre of the room he caught a glimpse of his white face in the mirror above the fireplace and scarcely recognised it as his own. He had closed the window not a moment too soon. Outside he heard the screaming reach an ultimate pitch of menace before merging into a great roaring sound as a mighty wind rushed down upon the house from the mountain. It struck with a force that made every door and window rattle; it was as though the house had been grasped and shaken by some gigantic hand. By this time John was on his knees upon the floor. The window blew in with a crash as the house was struck by a second and even more tremendous blow. Before he lost consciousness he remembered seeing the walls of the room suddenly bellying inwards and the lamp sliding from the table with a crash, plunging all into a chaotic darkness.

John awoke to feel the sun hot upon his face. The recollection of the previous night filled his mind with a sudden panic, and then the memory of that nightmare, if such it was, gradually receded. Yet still he hesitated to open his eyes; for if it was indeed a nightmare, then surely he would still be sitting in that Victorian chair in the farm parlour and not lying in the sun. On the contrary, if it had indeed been no nightmare he would be lying miraculously unhurt, amid the ruins of the farmhouse. At length, very warily, he opened his eyes and sat up.

He found himself lying on a smooth and gentle slope of close-bitten turf, his haversack, cape, boots and stockings upon the grass beside him. A little distance away to his left was a shapeless mound of grey stones, and beside this grew a clump of nettles and an ancient yew tree, sure signs of bygone human habitation. But of any recent ruin there was no sign whatever. The near-level slope where he sat formed the mouth of a steep cwm carved by a streamlet out of the mountain at his back, so that it formed a sort of natural amphitheatre from which he could look down over the valley below. There, directly beneath him, ran the swift flowing stream which he had crossed with such difficulty the previous night and there, up the opposite slope, was surely the gateway by which he had left the track over the pass, which he could see running diagonally along the opposite side of the valley. He shook his head in bewilderment as one who surfaces after a dive, not knowing where reality had ended and the dream had begun.

It was a perfect spring morning. The brilliant blue sky was flecked with innocent little cotton-wool cloudlets that drifted serenely along, the smaller ones dissolving as he watched them in the gathering heat of the sun. He saw their shadows moving along the slopes opposite, and noticed that above the screes and crags a more gentle slope extended upward towards the long, level skyline of the mountain ridge, a slope green with fresh bracken fronds and thickly populated with sheep and mountain ponies, many with small foals at heel. These higher slopes, made invisible by low cloud the previous night, now transformed the appearance of the valley. He watched a pair of buzzards soaring effortlessly on motionless moth-like wings upon an up-current of air above the crags opposite. Although the floor of the valley to his right was treeless, immediately to his left the stream disappeared in a little brake of alders, and he could see that beyond this the valley became progressively richer and well-wooded. There were glimpses of old farmsteads of pinkish grey stone or whitewash, and of blue pencils of woodsmoke spiralling upwards from morning fires.

So striking was the contrast between the beauty of the scene now spread before him and his first impression of the valley when seen from the head of the pass the previous evening, that John, although no philosopher, could scarcely avoid speculating upon it. What had appeared under that darkening stormlight to be so malign now seemed to have become wholly beneficent and of a heart-lifting beauty that seemed almost paradisial. Were good and evil purely human concepts, and did this little world that he surveyed include them both?

He put on his socks and boots, rolled up his cape and, shouldering his knapsack, set off down the valley. Within the first few yards he had struck a long-disused track which had obviously led into the mouth of the cwm and must have been the one he had found on scrambling up the bank the night before. He judged correctly that if he followed it he would ultimately join the main track at a point lower down the valley. He had only just regained the latter and begun to stride out towards Llanvethney when he saw coming towards him up the hill a Land Rover driven by a very worried-looking Alan Brett. On seeing John coming towards him apparently none the worse, Alan's face relaxed into a broad grin.

'Gosh, am I glad to see you!' he exclaimed as he drew up beside John, leaning over and opening the door on the passenger side. John threw his rucksack into the back and clambered in.

'Where did you tuck yourself away last night when that storm hit you?' Alan asked. 'I guessed you'd be at the Youth Hostel, and it was when I called there just now and found you weren't there that I began to get really worried.'

John made no immediate answer to his question, and such reticence was so unusual that Alan looked keenly at him and judged correctly that he should forego any further cross-questioning, leaving the story to come out in his friend's own good time. So without further comment he reversed the Land Rover into a gateway and the two drove on in companionable silence down towards Llanvethney Priory.

The further they went the more beautiful the valley became, the more luxuriant the meadows and trees along its floor and the more majestic the sweep and curve of the mountains that enclosed it. The lovelinesss all about him loosed John's tongue, and he tried haltingly to explain to his friend the extraordinary contrast between the valley as he saw it now and his first impression of it as he entered it by the high pass the night before. In reply, Alan chuckled. '"An angel satyr walks these hills",' he quoted.

'Who wrote that?' asked the other sharply.

'A chap named Francis Kilvert,' explained Alan. 'He was curate of Clyro, just the other side of the Wye, in the 1870s and used to do a lot of walking in these mountains. It appears, rather enigmatically, in the diary that he kept, which was published just before the last war.'

'I think I understand what he meant,' replied John after a short silence.

It was not until that evening, when the two friends were comfortably ensconced in deep armchairs on either side of a blazing log fire in the big drawing room of the Priory Hotel, that John told his old friend the whole strange story. Throughout, Alan listened with the utmost attention, never speaking a word until John had finished. Then, after a moment's silence, he asked, 'If I were to show you a large-scale map of the area, do you think you could pin-point the site of this mysterious farm where you stayed – or thought you stayed?'

'I am sure I could,' the other replied, whereupon his friend unfolded a map, two and a half inches to the mile, and spread it before them. It did not take John long before he had marked the spot with the point of a pencil. It was too easy; here was the line of the track descending from the pass, the stream running down almost parallel with it and, beyond it, the dense contour lines which marked the steep slope of the mountain. There was only one indentation in those contour lines, and that must surely indicate the steep little cwm in which he had found himself that morning.

No sooner had he marked the place than Alan exclaimed in an awed voice, 'I thought as much. Ty yr Deol!' Then, in answer to his friend's look of blank incomprehension, he explained, 'Ty yr Deol; that means "the house of vengeance".' He got to his feet, opened the doors of a large glass-fronted bookcase, searched for a moment, and then drew out a green-backed book.

'It's our friend Francis Kilvert again: he tells us all about it in his diary, volume one,' – he rifled through the pages – 'page two hundred and seventy-nine.' Alan quoted:

'Near Capel y Ffin at the mouth of a dingle on the mountain side stood the house of Ty yr Deol (the house of vengeance). Some crime had been perpetrated on the spot and the place was accursed. When the workmen were building the house they heard a voice which seemed to fall from the air and come down the dingle, saying, "Move the work across the green." "For why?" called back the astonished workmen. "The spot is accursed," said the voice solemnly. "For how long?" shouted the workmen. "Until the ninth generation," returned the voice. Three attempts were made to build the house. Twice the house fell. The third time the house was built. One night in winter a young man came up the mountain to court his sweetheart who lived in the Ty yr Deol, the accursed, ill-fated house. His greyhound whined at the door, hung back and refused to enter the house, and no coaxing would induce him to come in. The young man took it as a warning and returned home. That night there was a land-slip or a snow slip, or a sudden mass of snow melted down the dingle driving the ice and water before it. The accursed house was overwhelmed and swept away and everyone in the house perished.'

When Alan had read this the two friends sat for many minutes in silence, gazing into the flames of the fire, each busy with his own thoughts, while outside dusk thickened in the valley and the room grew dark except for the flickering fire-light.